ya
Kobayas
hi,
M
MAY 17 2010
Kobayashi, Miyuki.
Kitchen princess
c2009.
D0809020

Kitchen Princess

Search for the Angel Cake

Miyuki Kobayashi

Illustrations by Natsumi Ando

Translated by Karen McGillicuddy

BALLANTINE BOOKS

NEW YORK

A Del Rey Manga/Kodansha Trade Paperback Original

Published in the United States by Del Rey,
an imprint of The Random House Publishing Group,
a division of Random House, Inc., New York.

DEL REY is a registered trademark and the Del Rey colophon is a trademark of Random House, Inc.

Publication rights arranged through Kodansha Ltd.

First published in Japan in 2008 by Kodansha Ltd., Tokyo,
as *Kitchen no Ohime-sama ~Tenshi no Keki wo Sagase!~*

ISBN 978-0-345-51628-2

Original cover design by Akiko Omo. U.S. edition cover by Phil Balsman
Cover illustration: Natsumi Ando

Printed in the United States of America

www.delreymanga.com

2 4 6 8 9 7 5 3 1

Translator: Karen McGillicuddy

Book design by Mary A. Wirth

Contents

■

Spring / printemps

Recipe One • Najika and French Toast

■

1

"Kazami-san? I have a favor to ask."

"Huh?"

It was after class, in April.

I had just left my classroom and was walking down the hall when I suddenly heard her voice.

When I turned around, there she was: A girl as adorable as a cream puff covered in snow-white powdered sugar.

Petite and fair-skinned, she had long, flowing hair.

"Umm, you're Takanashi-san from the Special Class, right?" I asked.

"Yes. Anju Takanashi," she replied. She had a sweet voice like a tinkling bell.

She was such a shy girl, it was almost the first time we had ever spoken. What could she want from me?

"Kazami-san, you once had a part-time job at a cake shop, right?"

"Yeah. How'd you know?"

"I know everything about you, Kazami-san," she said.

"Huh?"

What did that mean?

"I would like to offer you a job."

"A job?"

"The cherry blossoms are supposed to be in full bloom this weekend, right?"

And then, almost unconsciously, the two of us turned to look out the window, the one that had such a wonderful view of the school yard.

The cherry trees were covered in flower buds.

A tender spring breeze swayed through the winter daphne blossoms. Confronted by the quick approach of spring, the bitter cold of winter disappeared as if it had never been. Just a few days ago, the trees had been barren. The flowers filling them seemed like a kind of magic.

"I would like to throw a flower-viewing party on Sunday in my garden. Would you make the refreshments and dessert for the party?" she asked.

"For how many people?"

"About ten, I think. But it's mainly going to be my parents and their friends."

"A group of adults? But you should ask a real caterer, not someone like me. . . ."

"No, I want to ask you, Kazami-san! It has to be you!"

Anju-chan gazed at me with shimmering eyes and squeezed my hand tightly in both of hers.

"Please! Just this once! I'll pay you for it, of course!"

Huh?

"Don't refuse, Najika-chan!"

W-why was she so serious about it?

I don't get i-i-it!

■ ■ ■

My name is Najika Kazami.

I'm in the middle school section at Seika Academy, a private school in Tokyo. The school has students from elementary up through high school—and it's full of rich kids.

I lost my parents in an accident, so I grew up at an orphanage called Lavender House. So how is it that I—a wild child from the great, wide open, where there aren't even any convenience stores or fast-food chains—got into a fancy school like this?

Well, the truth is, the top-ranked students in each grade belong to the "Special Class"; only the very best students are admitted to the Special Class.

The Special Class, in other words, is composed of students who excel in academics or sports or activities, and they can attend the school free of charge. I came to this school from Hokkaido as a special student.

And what's my exceptional talent?

It's cooking!

Unusual, isn't it?

Apparently Seika Academy is going to open a cooking school.

My dream is to become the best pastry chef in the world!

■ ■ ■

"What? Anju Takanashi?"

Daichi looked up from his coffee cup. We were in the Fujita Diner.

"You know her?"

"Yeah, we've both been here ever since elementary school. My dad's even taken me over to her house to

play. But she's so quiet, I've hardly ever actually spoken to her."

Daichi Kitazawa's father is the director of the school. Daichi's a tough kid with a short temper, and he's amazing at basketball. He also has a strong sense of what's right—he can be so kind and considerate of others.

"That place is creepy. It's like a horror movie."

Daichi's face twisted openly.

"Huh? What's so creepy about it?"

Akane, who was sitting beside Daichi, paused in the middle of eating her cake.

"Najika, they're a really good family. Both of her parents are incredibly famous."

"They are?"

"Her dad is Seiji Takanashi, the orchestra conductor. Her mom is Hiroko Takanashi, the pianist."

"Oh wow! Even I've heard of them, and I don't know anything about classical music! They're in commercials, right?"

Daichi shuddered.

"Her grandma is a famous pianist, too. She's terrifying. She's really uptight about manners. When we were eating, she told me I held my chopsticks badly and smacked my hand. Then she started giving me a lesson on how to use chopsticks right there. I couldn't believe it!"

"Oh my gosh," I said.

"Ever since then I've been scared and I swore I would never go near that place again. Plus, they made us listen to string trios, or classical concerts, or whatever, that went on forever. It bored me out of my mind."

"Plus, Anju's parents are both famous gourmets, Najika," Akane added.

Akane Kishida is a model. She's always on the cover of a teen fashion magazine called *Strawberry*.

She's thin and fair-skinned and has a cool sense of style. She's always fashionable. Her eyes are a little sharp and cat-like; they're really unique.

Even with my charm, she's on a whole different level from me, so we're pretty much exact opposites. When I transferred to this school, Akane didn't like me, but now, somehow, she's become my best friend.

"Will you be all right catering a flower-viewing party for a family like that?"

"Urk. I bet the old lady would get mad at me before the cooking starts."

"Just forget about it. No one'll hold it against you," Daichi said flatly.

"Well . . . about that . . . I already accepted, actually," I admitted.

"Wha-a-a-at?"

Akane was shocked.

"Are you crazy? Why would you rush into a promise like that?" Daichi shouted.

"Y-you don't need to yell about it. I wanted to get a job and earn enough money of my own to go back to Hokkaido for summer break."

"Well, maybe you can charm that scary old lady, Najika. This is you we're talking about, after all. Why not give it a try?"

Akane grinned.

"Akane, you're just enjoying the show, aren't you?"

"You noticed?"

But Daichi seemed truly concerned.

"Najika, really, you should get out of it. That old lady is trouble."

"But Anju-chan asked me with such big, watery eyes."

I mimicked Anju-chan's voice.

■ ■ ■

"I love the sweets you make, Kazami-san."

"Really?"

"Yeah. The cookies you handed out for Christmas one year and your strawberry shortcake were both some of the best things I'd ever tasted."

"Thank you."

"And your parents were famous pastry chefs, right? My grandmother had some of their food a long time ago. She told me it was incredibly good."

"Did she really?"

"And she said she wanted to experience that taste again."

My parents had both been pastry chefs before they died. My dad, Nanase Kazami, was a genius who made innovative desserts. And my mom, Kaori Kazami, was known as the best of the best for perfectly executing traditional sweets.

Yes, I'm the daughter of two people like that.

So ever since I was born, I've grown up surrounded by sweets.

■ ■ ■

"Anju-chan complimented my parents, so I accepted without thinking."

"You are so gullible, Najika. You fell for it completely. And that old lady's request? It might be a trap. It's so fishy!" Daichi seemed to be utterly opposed to it.

"You were tricked at the head of the PTA's house before, too," Akane murmured.

"Yeah."

"Go and tell them you can't do it. They can just get a top restaurant or hotel to cater for them! The family's stinking rich. Right?"

"A-all right. I'll go over to Anju-chan's house right now and tell her I can't do it."

2

■

"What? This?"

I had reached Anju-chan's house by following the map Daichi drew for me, but when I found myself actually standing in front of it, I gaped in surprise.

"W-wow!"

I had no idea she lived in a mansion like this! It was even more beautiful than I'd pictured! It was a huge, old-fashioned, Western-style building that looked very venerable.

Oh my gosh! It's incredible! It's so tasteful.

Compared to this place, Lavender House might as well have been a rabbit hutch.

Ugh . . .

Looks like I should have refused after all. Our backgrounds were just too different.

I rang the bell.

"Just a moment!"

Anju-chan popped out from behind the massive, sturdy wooden door.

"Oh! What is it, Najika-chan? You came over already? That's great!" she cried.

"Oh, uh, no, it's . . ."

"Come in! I'll show you the garden first."

"Um, actually, I—"

"I want to have the party here. We have garden parties all the time."

"Oh wow! This is great. It's so big!" I said.

"Isn't it nice?"

"It's incredible."

It was a *huge* lawn. There were green trees, and all kinds of flowers were blooming, including mimosas and lilacs.

And in the middle of it all stood a magnificent cherry tree. The cherry tree was covered with flowers, which gave it a faint pale-pink blush. It looked like the cherry blossoms would be seen in full bloom that weekend.

I let out a long sigh. I bet it was going to be amazing.

"That's a beautiful cherry tree."

"My grandfather loved it very much before he passed away. Let's go back inside."

"Oh, Anju-chan . . ."

Somehow, it had gotten way more difficult to refuse her request.

As I was stressing out, I took a step into the house and saw a long, dark brown hallway stretching ahead of me. Inside the house, it was perfectly still and the floor was chilly. There was a grand piano in the sitting room. Oil paintings decorated the walls and there were antique vases everywhere. The room had a high ceiling.

Everything about it was classic. It's like this spot was the only thing that had been secretly left behind by the flow of time.

And there wasn't the slightest sign that people lived there.

"Um, where are your parents?"

"They're both on tour in Europe. They're busy so they're usually not at home."

A sad look crossed Anju-chan's face.

"But they're both coming home this weekend. Here, have a seat."

I sat down on the expensive-looking leather sofa.

"Er, what about your grandmother?"

Where was the scary old lady everyone had told me about?

"Oh, my grandmother hasn't been doing very well lately."

Anju-chan sighed.

"She's taking a nap right now."

In the perfect silence, the big, old, decorative clock made a heavy ticking sound, counting out the seconds. The commotion of the city seemed a million miles away.

So Anju-chan had grown up in this quiet house, with her mom and dad often away.

She was always quiet and didn't express her wishes. She didn't assert herself. I felt like I now understood a little bit of the secret behind her personality.

"Here you go."

Anju-chan brought in a tea and cake set.

"Try it?"

"Oh, please don't go to any trouble . . ."

It was a thick chocolate cake, coated in glistening chocolate. And there was cream, lightly whipped, on the side. It had no frivolous decoration. It was a *serious*, grown-up cake, exactly like this house.

"Oh! Is this the cake that European nobility has called the best in the world, the Sacher-torte from the Sacher Hotel?"

"I'm not surprised you recognize it, Najika-chan. This is my mom and dad's favorite. They had it flown in specially from Vienna. Please, try some."

It would be shameless of me to accept since I had come to back out, but I couldn't resist!

"All right!"

Oh!

"This chocolate is so sweet it makes my teeth hurt. And the rough texture of the flour—this doesn't happen with Japanese flour. There's apricot jam between the layers; a little sour. And tying everything together is this fresh cream with no sugar in it."

"That's Najika-chan: the owner of an absolute sense of taste!"

Oh, so an "absolute sense of taste" is "the ability to know all the tastes in something without ever comparing it to anything and to never forget a taste once you've experienced it." It's also the ability to figure out the ingredients in something and how it was made.

Apparently I have that ability, but I don't really understand it very well myself.

"We have the whole cake, Najika-chan. Please, eat more."

"Um, do your parents always eat amazing cakes like this?"

"Yeah. They like everything that's high class."

There were small barbs behind her words.

"But even though they obsess over their food and their decorating, they neglect their daughter. They don't care about me."

"Uh, hey, Anju-chan—" I interrupted awkwardly. "Thanks a lot for letting me taste that. But I'm afraid I can't offer my sweets to adults with refined tastes like this. So thank you for asking me, but I think I have to decline."

"Please don't say that! You're amazing, Najika-chan. Everyone talks about you."

Anju-chan squeezed my hands tightly.

"Your sweets cured Akane-chan's eating disorder, didn't they?"

"Well, no, that was . . ."

"Your sweets made Sora-senpai and Daichi-kun get along again, didn't they?"

"I wouldn't go that far . . ."

"Anyway! I think there's some kind of magic in your sweets, Najika-chan. And if there is, then my family . . ."

"Your family what?"

Anju-chan stopped herself suddenly.

"Actually . . ." Anju-chan started again, speaking haltingly. "Flower-viewing parties are a fun annual event for my family. We hold them every single April. We invite relatives or members of the orchestra and have a nice garden party."

"Okay."

"But this year my parents said they weren't going to do it."

"What?"

"Because they're getting divorced. . . ."

"Divorced?!"

"But they said they're putting it off because my grandmother is sick. They said it would be bad for her health if she got a shock."

Anju-chan bit her lip.

"So if my grandmother dies, my whole family will be destroyed all at once. I don't want that to happen. Then I really will be all alone."

Tears trailed down her cheek, then began to fall more heavily. It was as if some sort of tension inside her had snapped.

"If I can do anything about it, I want to stop that from happening."

Anju-chan's small shoulders shook as she cried.

Earlier, I had felt jealous of Anju-chan for living in a wonderful house like this.

A gorgeous mansion. The best chocolate cake in the world. Famous musicians for parents.

I'd thought it was an ideal family. But I was an outsider and I didn't understand. They'd seemed so blessed, but I guess everyone has problems.

Lavender House is cramped and run-down, but everyone was always with me. Hagio-sensei didn't use the highest quality ingredients, but the stews and fresh-baked bread she made were delicious and the crowded dinner table was always lively.

I'd had so much, really.

My parents were gone, but I grew up surrounded by people who were more than family. I grew up in a place where smiles never faded.

And really, that's *true* luxury.

I couldn't think of anything to say, so instead I gently patted Anju-chan's trembling back.

"Ever since I was little, my parents have been flying all over the place for concerts overseas. So my grandmother raised me. She's strict about manners and about playing the piano. Didn't Daichi-kun or Akane-chan mention that?"

"Oh, well . . . a little."

"They told you she was scary, right? That's why everyone stopped coming over here."

Anju-chan smiled through her tears.

"But we had fun after my piano lessons. I would always drink tea with my grandmother and eat sweets. They were so good. But we can't do that anymore."

Anju-chan's face darkened again.

"What's wrong with your grandmother?"

". . . She didn't recognize me earlier."

"What?"

3

■

That means she has . . .

"Do you want to meet my grandmother, Najika-chan?"

Anju's grandmother was in a bright sunroom overlooking the garden. I was nervous. For some reason, I was even scared.

"Grandmother, this is my friend from school, Kazami-san."

"Pleased to meet you. My name is Najika Kazami."

The old lady looked up. She had white hair and was wearing a kimono, and was seated in a wheelchair. Her hair was tied back neatly and she was wearing a little makeup. *Wow, she's pretty.* I'd heard when she was younger she'd been a very popular, beautiful pianist.

"I feel as if this isn't the first time I've met you."

Her voice was brisk. She was elegant and had perfect posture, and she certainly didn't *look* like anything was wrong with her.

"You're Mr. and Mrs. Kazami's daughter, aren't you?"

"That's right."

"You look just like your father. Even your voice is like his."

"You met my father?"

"Yes, I have met your parents."

"Really?"

"I very much enjoyed their cakes. They were marvelous."

"Thank you so much!"

"It was so unfortunate, your parents' accident."

"Yes . . ."

"They were on their way to a competition, I believe?"

My parents, both sets of grandparents, and I, their only child, were headed by boat to Paris to participate in a worldwide dessert competition.

My mom and dad were always busy, and even though I understood, I'd been looking forward to a leisurely trip on the boat with them.

Along the way, the boat had an accident and I was the only one who made it.

So, I was left utterly alone.

Since my parents had been up-and-coming pastry chefs with a lot of attention focused on them, lots of media agencies followed me around trying to get a picture of the "tragic orphan."

The person who reached out to me in that moment was an old friend of my maternal grandmother's, Hagio-sensei. It was better to live quietly at her orphanage in Hokkaido than in Tokyo, where I was hunted by the media.

Hagio-sensei was the one who made that decision for me. That's why I was able to grow up serenely in Hokkaido. I'm truly grateful to Hagio-sensei, from the bottom of my heart.

Anju-chan gently took my hand.

"I've heard a lot about your parents from my grandmother. And about their daughter. So I was really interested in you, Najika-chan. You're always so cheerful and upbeat despite such a sad thing happening to you. I have always admired you from a distance."

"Oh, please don't say you admire me. But that's why you knew so much about me, huh?"

"I wanted to talk to you, but I'm so shy, all I could do was watch you."

There was someone who had been watching me. I never knew that.

But I was glad.

The old lady spoke up. "In fact, Kazami-san, I'd asked your parents to do something for me."

"You did?"

"They passed away without fulfilling their promise. So I wonder, as their daughter, would you keep the promise in their stead?"

"What sort of promise was it?"

"I wanted them to make a white cake I'd had as a teenager while I was abroad. That was what I asked them to do."

"A white cake? What was it?"

"It was fluffy, sweet, and extremely tasty."

"Fluffy?"

"It tasted like being in heaven. I simply must taste that cake once more."

A promise my mom and dad made long ago. I never

imagined I could run into them again in a place like this. It made me happy, somehow.

It felt like my mom and dad had been waiting for me in this house where time seemed to have stopped. In a special, delicious memory.

I had those, too. Of course, mine was a cake my parents had made for me. My dad fed me the freshly baked cake. My mom tenderly wiped the cream off my cheek.

I've been able to eat lots and lots of delicious sweets since I came to Tokyo. But for me, my mom and dad's will always be the best.

But my mom and dad are gone now. I can never eat their cake again. Of course I can re-create it with the same recipe. But my mom and dad can never make it for me again.

That makes me a little sad.

But I had a mom and dad who spoiled me. The taste of that cake is a very sweet taste, full of happy memories.

The white cake the old lady had eaten over fifty years earlier—I felt like I could understand why she wanted to taste it again. I wanted to make it for her. In my mom and dad's place.

"What kind of cake was it? Could you be a little bit more specific?"

"Let me see . . ."

The old lady thought about it deeply and fell silent for a long time.

After a while, she suddenly lifted her head.

"Have you remembered something?"

At my question, the old lady's face became suspicious.

"And who might you be?"

"Huh?"

What?

What just happened?

A chill ran down my spine.

"Grandmother, you should rest."

Anju-chan quickly laid a hand on her grandmother's shoulder.

"Yes, you're right. I'm a bit tired."

"I'm going to go put her to bed, Najika-chan. I'll be back."

■ ■ ■

A little while later, Anju-chan came back.

"I'm sorry. Did that shock you?"

I couldn't say anything.

"Usually she's all right, but sometimes she gets like this. It's like her memories get muddled up."

Tears glistened in Anju-chan's eyes.

"She looks the same as always, but bit by bit, it's like the grandmother I know is disappearing."

"Anju-chan!"

"After the flower-viewing party, please try to find the cake my grandmother said she wanted to taste again. I'm really sorry to ask you to do something like this."

"Don't be. I want to keep the promise my parents made."

"I feel that if she could eat that cake, the grandmother I know might come back. She might be happy again."

"It's all right. I'll find it! I know I will. Leave it to me!"

As I went back through the spring breeze, a cold wind blew up.

If I felt this shocked, how badly must Anju-chan's heart have been aching?

■ ■ ■

"I'm back."

When I returned to the Fujita Diner with a heavy heart, Daichi and Akane were waiting for me.

"Daichi! Akane!"

"We were worried. We've been waiting for you. I'm sorry I couldn't go with you. I just can't handle that old woman."

"And did you tell them you couldn't do it, Najika?"

"Daichi, Akane, I was kind of scared."

"I knew it. She's scary, right? Did they get mad at you?"

"It's not that. I . . ."

I couldn't find the words for the rest, and instead of words, tears flowed out of me.

■ ■ ■

"I can't believe that old hag could get sick . . ."

"And how can a perfect couple like that be getting a divorce? It'll be a huge scandal."

Daichi and Akane sighed at the same time.

"That's why I couldn't turn Anju-chan down."

"Okay, Najika. In that case, I'll help you out!"

"Daichi . . ."

"I'll lend a hand, too."

"Thank you, Akane!"

"But Daichi and I can't cook. You need someone who knows what they're doing to help, too."

Everyone stared at Fujita-san, who was sprawled on the sofa.

Fujita-san is the owner of the Fujita Diner.

He's a strange person: a talented chef who trained at Étoile, a three-star restaurant in France, but who, for some reason, is now working in this run-down school cafeteria. He's got a stubbly beard, is always lying around, and has zero drive. To put it another way, he's eccentric.

"Why me? I don't wanna!" Fujita-san refused immediately, exactly as we thought he would.

"It's an act of charity, Fujita-san!" Akane scolded him.

"I make it a policy not to interfere in people's family issues."

"You boss Najika around all the time. You tellin' me that you're not gonna help her out this once? Najika, starting tomorrow don't help him ever again!" Daichi shouted.

"All right. Thank you for everything you've done for me, Fujita-san."

I bowed my head and started to leave when—

"Freeze!"

Fujita-san leapt up from the couch.

"Hold it right there! Fine, I get it. I got no choice." He gave the green light reluctantly.

The tactic was a success. Daichi, Akane, and I winked at one another.

"What do you think would be a good menu for a flower-viewing party, Fujita-san?"

"I'd like to drink away the afternoon with some wine and cheese."

"Try to be serious!"

"Sake is good, too, if it's a Japanese menu."

"Quit jokin' around, old man!" Daichi advanced on him.

"This is why kids are no fun. It's going to be for adults, right? And if they do a lot of performances overseas, it really oughtta be Japanese food. Seasonal ingredients will have a richer taste and way more nutrients. Spring vegetables with wild plants, or clams and seaweed. Maybe broad beans with cabbage, or rape blossoms with green peas. Rice with bamboo shoots or hand-rolled sushi would be good, too. 'Japan is so great. Cherry blossoms are so great.

Family is so great.' You wanna make 'em think that, right?"

"I knew you would inspire me! You're so dependable, Fujita-san. Thank you!"

And soon, Sunday arrived. . . .

4

It was the day of the flower-viewing party.

The four of us—Fujita-san, Daichi, Akane, and I—headed to Anju-chan's house with a lot of ingredients we'd stocked up on the day before.

"Whoa! Hey, this garden is amazin'!"

Fujita-san had never been here before and his mouth hung open in surprise.

A sweet, gentle spring breeze wafted over the spacious green lawn. The new budding leaves shone in the brilliant light of the afternoon. Visiting birds sang as if celebrating the full bloom of spring. The sky was light blue. The clouds were faint, like cotton candy stretched ver-r-ry thin.

Then there was the star of the day, the cherry tree in full bloom.

The branches, covered in vibrant pink flowers, filled the sky, claiming the moment for their peak.

"Okay! We'll feed 'em the very best food and make those celebrities say it's great."

"Hey, you're pretty fired up, huh, Fujita-san?"

"That's 'cause I'm the son of a small-time cake-maker. You think I'm gonna lose as a representative of the common people?"

"All right! It's on!"

■ ■ ■

"Please bring the food out soon."

Fujita-san, Daichi, and Akane were getting the food ready in the kitchen when Anju-chan came in.

She was dressed in her best clothes today: an elegant dress with a white collar.

"Oh, Anju-chan, do you mind if I use these baguettes over here?"

"Oh, I don't think those are good anymore. My parents eat baguettes every morning, but those are stale, aren't they?"

"What a waste. Do you always throw them away, then?"

"Yes. You can't finish a whole one, after all."

Oh really? I suddenly got a great idea!

■ ■ ■

"Sorry to keep you waiting."

The four of us served the food to the guests.

Colorful hand-rolled sushi. Tempura of wild greens. Rape blossoms pickled in soy sauce. Fried egg rolled with shrimp and clover. Sesame seed tofu. Boiled beans, asparagus, and bamboo shoots.

When we brought out the lacquered lunch boxes, filled with an abundance of dishes using spring ingredients, the guests gave out cries of joy.

"My, how extravagant!"

"This is amazing! It's nothing but spring flavors."

"Yes, and it tastes good, too."

"And Anju-chan organized all this. Amazing."

Anju-chan blushed as everyone complimented her.

"Najika-chan, this is my mom and dad."

Anju-chan brought her parents over to me.

"H-hello. I'm Najika Kazami."

"Thank you for all this."

"Oh, don't mention it."

"This food is wonderful."

"You've helped us fully appreciate spring in Japan."

Anju-chan's parents were genuinely pleased as they thanked me.

But, oh, was I nervous! To think that *celebrities* like them were thanking *me*!

Not only that, Anju-chan's parents were both truly beautiful people. They were as flawlessly gorgeous as movie stars.

Oh, no, I'm going to lose it . . .

"Admiring the cherry blossoms and eating this Japanese food makes me feel like Japan is truly wonderful. Eating does more than simply fill one's stomach. It also fills one's heart," Anju-chan's mother said, with real feeling.

"Yes. Being able to eat seasonal foods with friends and family like this . . . that might be the greatest luxury of all," her father replied. "We haven't made enough time for family."

They both looked up at the cherry blossoms. Petals

began fluttering down from the tree. They rained from the sky onto people's hair and shoulders.

"Anju's parents seem pretty happy, don't they, Najika?" Daichi whispered in my ear.

"There! Exactly like I said!" Fujita-san murmured self-importantly.

"And the food is getting excellent reviews, too! Isn't that great, Najika?"

Akane clapped me on the shoulder.

"Of course it is. I made it, didn't I? Looks like French cuisine isn't the only thing I can do. My Japanese food works, too. I really am a genius," Fujita-san declared as he nodded self-assuredly. "All that's left is the dessert."

The guests were murmuring to one another.

"I can't wait for the dessert."

"I wonder what it will be."

"It has to be something terribly sophisticated."

Anju-chan came over to me.

"Najika-chan, we're ready."

"Okay. I'll go prepare the dessert."

"The cherry mochi and leaf mochi I made are works of art. Good work, Najika. You can take it from here!"

Saying this, Fujita-san started chugging down champagne gleefully.

"Hey, man!" Daichi yanked at Fujita-san's shirt.

"It's all right, Daichi. Thank you so much for helping today. You and Akane can go ahead and join in the flower viewing now."

"What, don't you need help, Najika?"

"It's fine. I can handle it from here."

■ ■ ■

"Sorry to keep you waiting!"

I put the plates onto a silver tray and went back into the garden.

"Here's today's dessert," I said.

"Huh? Hey, Najika!" Daichi had a horrified look on his face as he ran over to me.

"Are you crazy? What're you doing?"

Fujita-san came rushing over, too.

"Najika! I thought we prepared a *Japanese* dessert? What are you thinking? This doesn't go with Japanese food!"

"It'll be fine. So both of you just be quiet!" I cried.

"Huh?"

"Oh, a Western dessert? How unexpected. I

thought we'd be having some Japanese treat, or perhaps some fancy fruits." Anju-chan's mother smiled.

"Actually, I made this from the stale baguettes you left in the kitchen," I explained.

"What?!" Her mother and father were shocked.

"It's from our kitchen? That hard old bread?"

"Why? We were going to throw that out. You can't serve something like that to our guests. Take it away."

The other guests were frowning openly.

"What's going on?"

"Did she say she made that dessert with *bread they were going to throw away*?"

I turned to face Anju-chan's mom and dad.

"French toast is called *pain perdu* in French. It means 'lost bread.' In other words, bread that you can't eat anymore."

"Yes, I know. I've lived in Paris before." Anju-chan's mother smiled coldly.

"French toast is a recipe that was created to make stale bread good again."

"But in our home, we throw away stale bread," she said.

"Please just try it anyway."

"I'm sorry, but please take it away." Her mother pushed away the plate I held out to her.

"Well, *I'm* going to have some!"

Anju-chan seized the plate from my hands.

"I also prepared fresh cream, sour cream, powdered sugar, maple syrup, and homemade strawberry jam. There's a lot of fresh berries, too. Try mixing it with the things you like."

"All right. Here we go!"

Anju-chan took a bite.

". . . Wow! It's delicious!"

"Isn't it?"

"It's much better than normal French toast!"

"I used fresh, homemade butter that I made myself. The milk is fresh from this morning and the eggs were just laid, too," I said.

"Wow, homemade butter? That's fancy."

"Maybe I'll try a bite, then."

One or two of the guests took a plate.

"Oh! It's great!"

"This is absolutely exquisite!"

"They're right. I can't believe this was made from stale bread."

"Oh, which one?"

"It's true: This is more delicious than I expected. The flavor is exquisite."

"The surface of the bread is crisp but the inside is moist."

"Wow, I never knew French toast could be this good."

"Mom, Dad, try a bite! Please!"

"Anju . . ."

Anju-chan's parents reluctantly took a bite.

The next moment . . .

The two looked over at each other in amazement.

"It really is . . ."

"Oh my. It's delicious . . ."

All *right*! I did a victory dance in my heart. I was so happy I wanted to leap for joy.

"But nevertheless, there was no need to serve something like this on a day like today."

"I decided to serve this *because* it was a day like today," I said.

"What?"

"I wanted to show you that if you soak it in lots of fresh milk and eggs and fry it in fragrant butter, even rock-hard bread that you're thinking of throwing away can become something this delicious."

They were struck silent.

"We throw everything out so easily. We toss things aside if there's anything even slightly wrong with them. But don't you think that's a waste?"

Her mother and father remained quiet. Anju-chan stared intently at them both.

"I wanted you to take another look at it before you threw it out. Because Anju-chan planned this party to communicate that to you two."

"Anju . . ."

"Is that what this is about?"

Anju-chan's eyes were wet with tears.

5

"Mom, Dad, please don't get a divorce. Please try to make things better again."

Tears rushed to Anju-chan's eyes and the three embraced tightly.

"I don't want you to do that."

"Anju—"

Her father smiled as he stroked Anju-chan's hair.

"Not even stale bread should be thrown away if it can be turned into something so delicious."

Anju's mother nodded, too. "Yes, exactly."

"I wonder when we developed the habit of throwing things away just like that."

Her father looked up. "Thank you, Kazami-san. I'm sorry for the terrible things my wife and I said to you."

"It's okay. You should thank Anju-chan, not me."

As I bowed my head, tears filled Anju-chan's mother's beautiful eyes.

"I'm sorry, Anju. We must have hurt you."

Thank goodness. Really, thank goodness.

My heart swelled with emotion. Relief, joy, and the sense of satisfaction you feel after a job well done spread through my entire body.

"I see. So the rejuvenation of bread they were going to throw out stands for the rejuvenation of the family that had decided to divorce," Daichi murmured. "The message was 'please don't throw away your family, your home, so easily,' huh?"

"Yeah."

"Way to go, Najika."

"Yes, well done."

A voice spoke behind me and I turned around, surprised. At some point, the old lady had come up directly behind me in her wheelchair.

"Augh! It's her!"

Daichi recoiled.

"Well, imagine that! Treating people as if they were monsters. Why, isn't that the younger Kitazawa boy?"

Daichi had been trying to get away, but he suddenly turned back around with a cringe.

"I-it's been awhile! H-how have you been, ma'am?"

"Well now! Before you could barely say hello. You've become a bit more adult, I see," the old woman said.

"Uh! Y-yes ma'am. Thank you," Daichi fumbled.

There was something weird about this. He'd rebelled against his father so fiercely—but there were people that even Daichi couldn't butt heads with.

"Kazami-san, may I have some French toast, as well?" she asked.

"Yes, of course!"

I handed a plate to her.

"How is it?"

"I've never had such delicious French toast."

The old lady smiled.

"It feels as if the taste is spreading throughout my body. You certainly are the daughter of famous pastry chefs."

"Thank you so much!"

"The weather today is very pleasant, isn't it? On a day like this, it's easy to understand how food can change our lives."

Yes. The things we ate today will become part of our

bodies. They will become blood, bones: our lives. That's why I want to eat delicious food every day.

The sweet scent of the flowers tickled the tip of my nose. The flower petals fluttered down, dancing over everyone's smiling faces.

Spring is such a beautiful season. It feels like all suffering and bad things will disappear forever. Flowers bloom from withered branches. Green buds push out of the frozen earth.

That strong will to live: Spring is the season of rejuvenation. And it's the season of beginnings.

I hoped that everyone could forget about everything that's happened up until now and start over again from here . . .

"Najika-chan—"

Anju-chan came up beside me.

"Teach me how to make French toast, too. I want to make it again for my mom and dad so that we never forget how we felt today."

"Okay! How about tomorrow at the Fujita Diner?"

"After classes, okay?"

The family sat together and all ate the same meal. That adds a flavor more powerful than any spice.

And when you eat good food, you can be happy. You become cheerful. Your strength grows.

Being alive becomes fun. Eating is living. Living is eating.

"Najika-chan, please try to find my grandmother's white cake."

"Of course! Leave it to me! I have a couple of ideas."

"You would!"

"Hey, Najika-chan? I've never had a friend before."

"Huh?"

"I had piano lessons every day, so I never had a friend I could open up to. But do you mind if I think of you as a friend from now on?"

"But I already consider you a friend, Anju-chan," I said.

"Really?"

Anju-chan's large eyes, like bubbling springs, glistened as tears gathered in them once more.

Her pure smile rippled beautifully across her face.

"Then will you call me just 'Anju'?" she asked.

"Okay. And you can call me Najika, Anju."

"Okay!"

"Najika! Nice work! We took our share of the flower-viewing lunch boxes. Let's eat them together!"

Akane held out a lacquered box.

"Trust you to think of that, Akane! You're so smart! What should we eat first?"

"I'm eating the beef first!" she said.

"What? You remember today's theme? You're destroying the mood of spring."

"I always eat the things I want to eat first. Even if it *is* a flower-viewing party, I'm in the mood for meat!"

"You always do things your way, huh?" I laughed.

"You could also say she doesn't know how to appreciate the occasion."

Daichi laughed.

"Excuse me?!"

"I'll have some beef, then."

"Daichi! You're so mean!"

Everyone's laughter floated up into the spring air.

■ ■ ■

What should I eat tonight? I get excited just thinking about it.

Eating is something positive. Eating is a hope for the future.

And what will I eat tomorrow?

Before I realized it, the first star of the evening was shining beyond the cherry branch.

In the lavender-colored twilight.

"Anju!"

When they called for her, Anju ran over to her mother and father.

And the three shadows stretching out in the setting sun became one. The cherry petals were lifted by everyone's emotions and danced up into the gorgeous spring evening.

It was like a confetti of blessings.

One • Spring • French Toast
TIP FROM NAJIKA
Even stale bread can be made fluffy again! Try this recipe with different kinds of bread. Of course, you can also make this without cutting the bread into little pieces. Adjust the amount of sugar to your taste!
INGREDIENTS • 1 serving
• Baguette . . . 6 inches (or one slice of thickly sliced bread)
• Egg yolk . . . 1
• Sugar . . . 1 tbsp
• Milk . . . 1/3 cup
• Butter . . . 1 tbsp
• Powdered sugar . . . to taste
INSTRUCTIONS
1
Cut the baguette into one-inch squares.
2
Combine the egg yolk, sugar, and milk in a bowl, and whisk until combined.
3
Add the pieces of baguette to step 2 and soak up plenty of the egg mixture throughout the bread.
4
Heat a frying pan and add butter. When the butter has melted, add the pieces of baguette from step 3 and fry over medium heat until golden. Turn and fry the other side.
5
Arrange on a plate and sprinkle with powdered sugar, or whatever you want, to finish. You can also serve with cinnamon, maple syrup, jam, or sliced fruit.
HONEY
JAM
DONE

Summer / été

Recipe Two • Najika and Milk Sherbet

■

1

"The trees on this road are amazing! It's like something out of *Anne of Green Gables*! Is this Prince Edward Island?" Anju's eyes sparkled.

"No, it's Hokkaido!"

The sharp answer came, of course, from Akane.

"That's in Canada, right? Of course this isn't it. We didn't need passports, for one thing." This comment, which missed the point completely, was from Daichi, who didn't have a clue about the romanticism of girls.

"Oh, you grew up in such an amazing place, Najika!"

The one in raptures, identifying with the heroines of stories, was Anju.

"But it feels so incredible, doesn't it?"

The cool, refreshing air. The clear blue sky peeping

through the leaves when we raised our eyes. The splash of light.

The warbling of birds. The scent of wet earth. The fields of lavender that went on forever.

The breeze blowing over the fields. The forest visible in the distance. A stand of birch trees. The surface of a lake as still as a blue mirror.

Hokkaido was bursting with light and colors you just don't see in Tokyo.

When I'd decided to go back to visit Lavender House for summer vacation . . .

"I want to go, too!"

"Me too!"

"Then I do, too!"

. . . these three had attached themselves to me.

We were planning to join up later with Seiya, who had gone home to Hokkaido ahead of us.

Seiya Mizuno is from Hokkaido, too. Like me, he came to Seika Academy as a special student in cooking. But unlike me, he is an heir: to the Mizuno Group, which manages resort hotels all across Hokkaido.

"Oh my gosh! It's a squirrel!" Anju shouted. "There's a fox! It's so cute!"

Anju was usually quiet and reserved, but now she was gushing.

"Hey, Najika? Do we have to walk much farther? Aren't there any buses?" Akane was already faltering.

"Nope," I responded instantly as we cut across a road.

"Aren't you giving up a little too easily, Akane?"

"Let's hail a cab. I can't go another step."

"We're not going to see any cabs."

The green leaves of a cornfield rustled dryly.

We turned at that corner and . . .

"Look, there it is. I can see it now!"

Standing in the middle of the field was a wooden building: Lavender House. It is an institution for children without parents or who, for whatever reason, couldn't stay with their families. I grew up here.

"I know you described it to us, but it really is run-down," Akane said sharply.

"No it's not! It's adorable! It's like *Little House on the Prairie*! Yay!"

Anju loved reading. And she loved girls' stories even more! She loved ribbons and lace and needlepoint. Teddy bears and anything European.

Today, too, she was dressed in a girly style like her heroine, Anne of Green Gables, in a dress and a straw hat, and was carrying a basket on her arm. It was a really cute outfit and well suited to Hokkaido and the outdoors.

"Your outfit is really something else, Akane! How can you wear all black?"

"I have to! Suntans are strictly forbidden for models!" Akane said.

Geez. Akane was wearing a black hat, black sunglasses, and a black long-sleeve jacket, and carrying a black parasol. Plus she had on black gloves—the total UV-prevention outfit. The midsummer sun was beating down on us, though.

"You're not one to discuss fashion, Najika!"

I was wearing a T-shirt and jean shorts.

"But in Hokkaido, it's more important to be able to move around easily!" I said.

I glanced over at Daichi beside me.

Of course I was excited to be taking a trip with Daichi, but maybe this wasn't the time for that.

"Just looking at you gives me heat stroke, Akane. Why don't you wear all-white instead of black?"

Daichi smirked.

colle
BLUE
LOVE
BLUE

"Black blocks the ultraviolet light better than white does! Every model knows that!" Akane argued, dripping with sweat.

Laughing, Anju pointed ahead.

"Oh! The children are lining up in front of Lavender House! It's been so long, they can't wait for you to come home, Najika."

"That's so true. Everyone pushes around me shouting 'Najika! Najika!' It's such a pain! They grab me and hug me as soon as they see me coming."

"You sound pretty happy about something that's such a pain," Daichi laughed.

"Well, I really *am* pretty happy."

I waved my arms and the children shrieked and came running.

"I'm back, every—"

"Ya-a-ay! It's Akane-chan!"

"It's Akane Kishida!"

"It's really her!"

"Whoa!"

"Can I have your autograph?"

Everyone thundered past me and crowded around Akane.

"Huh?"

My jaw dropped. I was shocked.

Plus, there was even a banner hanging over the entrance to Lavender House that said "Welcome, Akane Kishida-chan!"

Hu-u-uh? What a shock! *What about me, you guys?*

"Akane is really popular, huh?"

Anju was surprised, too.

"Heh-heh-heh. Seriously. This is incredible. They're ignoring Najika?"

Daichi was laughing, as if he was enjoying it.

"Hmmmmmph."

"Hey! Welcome back, Najika!"

Someone slapped my shoulder. It was . . .

"Futa! Thank you. How've you been?"

"Good."

"Hey—you've grown a lot," I said.

"I know! Here, I'll take your bag, Najika."

"Oh, how considerate! Can you take Anju's bag, too, then?"

"Sure thing."

"And mine."

Daichi slung his bag heavily onto Futa's shoulder, grinning.

"You can carry your own, Daichi! You're a man!"

Futa had been at Lavender House only a few years, but he was like my little brother.

"You don't want to get Akane's autograph?"

"I don't care about that stuff. Besides, it's the middle of summer. What's she doing dressed all in black? Models from Tokyo are too weird. When I first saw you guys coming, I thought you had a brown bear with you, Najika."

"A brown bear?! Ahahaha!"

Daichi burst out laughing.

"That's enough now."

We left Akane and the kids behind and went inside Lavender House, and there we saw a girl reading a book, all by herself in a corner.

She was a scrawny little girl with braids in her hair. She was cute, with big eyes and freckles. She was like a real-life Anne of Green Gables.

"I've never seen her before. Is she new?" I asked Futa.

"Yeah, she came last month. She's in fourth grade, like me."

I see. She'd just arrived, so she hadn't adjusted yet.

"Hello, I'm Najika Kazami. It's nice to meet you."

The girl was silent and didn't look up from her book. Hm—this was going to be tough.

"And what's your name?"

"Mai," she answered curtly.

"Mai-chan? That's a cute name. What does it mean?"

"It doesn't mean anything, It's just Mai," Mai-chan said, standing up to glare at me.

Huh?

"Hey! Why are you acting like that? You're being rude to Najika!" Futa shouted.

Mai-chan turned her face away roughly, then ran from the room.

"She's got some nerve!"

"Just like you when you first got here, Futa," I said.

"I wasn't that bad!" Futa frowned. "But that was pretty stupid of you, Najika."

"What was?"

"Asking her about the thing she's most sensitive about."

"I did?"

"Her name means 'rice.'"

"Rice?"

"It's written with the character for rice and it's pronounced 'Mai.'"

"Mai-chan, meaning rice, huh? That's a great name!" I said.

"What? It's *rice.* That's a weird name!"

"Futa! You're teasing her," I scolded.

"No I'm not! She's a really awful kid!"

"There must be good things about her, too."

"I dunno. I've never really talked to her."

"See? What do you know if you've never even talked to her?"

"Er—"

"Besides, Futa, you can tell a lot about a person's character by what they say about other people."

"Character? I don't really get what you mean."

"It means, calling people names makes the person calling names look worse."

"But everyone else says the same thing!"

"Everyone else says it? That's why you insult her? Without knowing anything about her?" I asked.

"You're mean, Najika! I haven't seen you in so long, and you're just lecturing me!"

Futa got angry and ran out of the room, too.

"Najika, is everything all right?"

Anju looked concerned.

"It's fine. I know Futa will understand."

"I hope so . . ."

"When I first came here, I didn't talk to anyone for a long time, either," I said.

"Huh? *You?*" Anju was surprised.

"Najika had just lost her parents, and owing to the shock, she couldn't talk, she didn't eat; she just cried by herself every day," came a voice behind us. I turned around and Hagio-sensei was standing there.

My beloved Hagio-sensei. The person I respected more than any other.

"Welcome home, Najika."

"Hagio-sensei!"

I hugged her.

My eyes teared up in happiness.

"I'm so glad to see you!"

"I'm happy, too. Now, Najika, it's a bit sudden, but I'd like to talk with you about Mai. Do you have a moment?"

2

■

"Mai doesn't eat much. She's very finicky and doesn't eat anything I offer her." Hagio-sensei was making me some cold buckwheat tea in the kitchen.

Ch-ring, ch-ring. The wind chime hanging from the eaves made a refreshing sound.

"I'd like you to do something about that with your special power, Najika."

"What happened to bring her here?"

"Her mother passed away early on. It was just her and her father, and then he died, too. She was moved around from one relative to another after that. Then we took her in."

"I see . . ."

My heart squeezed tight. Mai-chan's image overlapped with my own from long ago.

"I hate to ask, Najika, but would you see to Mai?"

"I'll handle it! There's something I want to talk to you about, too, Hagio-sensei."

"What's that?" she asked.

"Anju's grandmother is a former pianist named Fujiko Takanashi."

"Oh, yes, I know all about her. In our day, there was no one who didn't know who she was. She was a very popular pianist."

Anju smiled happily at Hagio-sensei's words.

I explained the current situation in detail.

■ ■ ■

After the flower-viewing party, every Sunday I made a different cake that I had guessed at from the hints "white and fluffy," and took it to Anju's house.

The first of them was a meringue pie. Next was white chocolate mousse.

Marshmallow cake. Vanilla soufflé. Yogurt cake. Coconut cake. Panna cotta. Bavarian cream cake. Milk jelly. And, finally, a trifle made only of white cream.

In the end, they were all wrong, but the old lady ate them all with pleasure and, most important, I really enjoyed the afternoon teatimes I spent surrounded by flowers in that green garden.

"My grandmother has really held herself together and been cheerful since you came, Najika," Anju had told me.

Sometimes Anju's mother and father, and even Akane, participated in our afternoon teas.

Even Daichi had come, but only once.

Only Fujita-san had refused to come, even though we invited him. (I'm so mad at him!)

The fresh, beautiful greenery, the sweet scent of flowers, the wind skimming across the table.

Fragrant tea. Laughter. Delicious sweets.

It was so peaceful and soft at those times that I found myself wishing it could continue forever.

■ ■ ■

"I see. So you want to make sure that she tastes that cake, then." Hagio-sensei sighed.

"You two are close to the same age, so I thought you might have a guess."

Anju looked intent, too, as she listened.

Hagio-sensei smiled suddenly, as if she'd remembered something. "When we were teenagers, there still weren't that many kinds of sweets in Japan and we didn't have the sort of information we have now. Strawberry shortcake was the greatest of luxuries for us."

"Wow."

"It's true. So the first time I tasted cheesecake, I was truly impressed. At that time, it was enjoying a small boom among young girls, even in Japan."

"White cheesecake . . . hm. I still haven't made a no-bake cheesecake!"

"It might be that!"

"Thank you, Hagio-sensei. That is a good guess!"

"Thank you very much." Anju bowed her head.

Just then, the door clattered open and Akane came in.

"Akane, why is your hair all messed up?"

"I'm exhausted! Those kids were all over me! They snatched off my hat and sunglasses."

"It's better this way, Akane. You look cooler." Daichi winked at me.

"Akane and Anju are staying at Seiya's father's hotel tonight, right?"

"No, I'm fine here!" Anju answered without any hesitation.

"Are you sure?"

"I want to see what it's like sleeping in a room under the roof! I feel like Sara from *A Little Princess.*"

Anju's eyes had gone dreamy again.

"Besides, it's full of kids here, so it's cheerful and fun."

"So you're going to do that, Anju? Oh, but you can go to the hotel, Akane."

"I'll stay here, too!"

"Huh?"

"After a welcome like that, I can't refuse to stay here just because it's run-down, can I?"

Hey, was Akane blushing?

She still held her head high, but deep down she was pleased by the children's pure-hearted affection for her.

"They heard you, Akane," Daichi said, and Akane spun around. The door was open a crack and a pile of children were gazing at her through it.

"Urk! I didn't mean it! It's not run-down, really!"

It was funny to watch Akane backpedaling.

■ ■ ■

After a lively dinner, cooked by Hagio-sensei, we spread a mat out in the room under the roof to make a simple bed. The three of us, Anju, Akane, and I, lay down on it together. Daichi was staying in the boys' room with Futa and the others.

"This is fun! It's like a school trip!" Anju seemed truly happy.

On the other side of the window, countless stars sparkled in the black velvet of the night sky.

"Wow. It's beautiful. It feels like the stars are going to start raining down on us."

The stillness of the quiet night. The pale light was the shining Milky Way. The Summer Triangle. The Big Dipper.

The three of us were quiet for a while, gazing up at the summer constellations.

Anju broke the silence.

"I'm sorry, Najika."

"For what? Why are you apologizing all of a sudden?" I asked.

"My grandmother's memory loss has been getting worse lately. . . . She can't explain herself clearly. It's causing you all kinds of trouble."

"It's fine. Searching through lots of different desserts and making them is great practice for my future. Besides, your grandmother always pays me for the cakes."

"That's true. And Najika was able to come home to Hokkaido with the money she's made so far," Akane added.

"That makes me feel better."

There were dark silhouettes of trees on a hilltop. The hooting of an owl from the forest. The yellow crescent moon.

"Oh! A shooting star!"

"Make a wish, Najika."

"I wish that I can find your grandmother's white cake soon."

The night air was like pale gelatin. The stars rained down like sparkling confetti candy. The three of us fell asleep instantly, as if under a spell.

And that night I had a dream about winning a white-cake-eating contest.

■ ■ ■

"Good morning!"

When I opened the window, the cool morning air of Hokkaido rushed in. The fresh scent from the purple

lavender fields. The high, blue sky, unmarred by power lines.

And the green grass bent in the summer wind, shining silver.

Breakfast with the kids—with pancakes, homemade jam, and fresh milk.

"That was great!"

Just as we'd finished eating . . .

"Hey! Morning, guys!" Seiya came over.

"Oh, Seiya! You're just in time."

"Oh really? Were you waiting for me, Najika?"

"We just need a hand. Okay, everyone! This morning you're doing your homework!"

"Wha-a-at?"

There was a storm of booing from the kids.

"In exchange, you get Najika's special summer vegetable curry rice for lunch!"

"Hurray!"

"All *right*!"

"I love Najika's curry!"

"Okay, then, here I go! Futa and Mai-chan, you're my gofers!"

"What? Me and Futa-kun? Where are we going?" Mai-chan's expression tensed.

"We have to get the ingredients for the curry ready!" I said.

"At the grocery store?"

"No way. In the vegetable fields right outside," I explained.

"Huh?"

3

■

"Augh!!"

As we were gathering vegetables in the field, Akane suddenly screamed.

"What's wrong?"

"It's a worm! Eeek!" she cried out.

"The worm proves this is good soil. This is why being raised in a city is a problem," I said.

"Ack! It's a weird bug!" Seiya screamed, too, from the other side.

"I didn't know natives of Hokkaido could be that delicate, too. How sad . . ." I sighed.

In contrast . . .

"Najika, look how many potatoes I got!"

"And I got all these tomatoes!"

Daichi and Anju were covered in mud, but they seemed to be having fun.

Daichi was even barefoot, harvesting the potatoes with real resolution. It was somehow reassuring. He had made up completely with Futa and they were getting along like brothers.

"Futa, you're in charge of carrots, okay? We're counting on you."

"Got it!"

"Mai, you're in charge of onions."

"Oh. Mai hates onions. She can't eat them at *all*. Ha ha ha," Futa laughed.

"Are you talking about yourself? You always pick out the carrots!" Mai said.

"I'll eat them today!"

"Me too!"

"Don't fight!" I warned them. Then . . .

"I'm tired of this! I'm going back to the house." Mai-chan glared sharply at me and threw away her work gloves.

"All right. But first, try this freshly picked tomato." I held a tomato out to her.

"It's not dirty."

Mai-chan brought it to her lips hesitantly. "Wh . . . it's sweet."

"See? Aren't fresh vegetables incredible?"

Mai-chan didn't answer.

"The food we eat every day—what is it like before it becomes *food*? What does it look like before it's stocked on the supermarket shelves? I bet you didn't know. When you find that out, you start to feel truly grateful for it, and when you eat, the food tastes even better. That's why I invited you today, Mai-chan."

Mai-chan said nothing and bowed her head to me, then went back down the road we'd come down.

"Hey! She doesn't want to help us or what?" Futa started to run after her, but Daichi stopped him. "Leave it, Futa."

"But . . ."

"She understands. She'll behave better soon," Daichi said.

I nodded slowly at Daichi's words.

■ ■ ■

When we got back to the house, we started making the curry in the kitchen.

First we sautéed the curry powder with lots of spices, and the children started gathering in the kitchen, drawn there by the smell.

"Man, it looks great!"

"Let me, let me!"

Everyone wanted to help.

I was like that, too, when I was a kid.

"Najika, I'm making the curry. Can you help?"

"Coming!"

When Hagio-sensei asked me to help, I sort of felt like I was everyone's big sister.

"You're really good at using a kitchen knife, huh, Najika?"

It made me so happy when people complimented me.

Looking back on it now, I realize I might have been in the way, but Hagio-sensei was patient and let me help out anyway.

"Can you peel the carrots and potatoes for me?"

"Okay!"

I also called out to Mai-chan, who was reading a book.

"Come help, too, Mai-chan."

She didn't answer.

"You can just peel the onions you picked earlier, Mai-chan. That's enough."

Again, there was no answer.

I gave up and returned to the kitchen. I had just started mincing the onion when Mai-chan appeared silently beside me.

Then she picked up the knife without a word and started smoothly mincing the onion.

"Wow, that's impressive. You're really good," I commended her.

"My dad was a chef. . . ." Mai-chan said haltingly. "I always helped him."

"Oh, I get it. That's why you're called Mai-chan, huh?" I said.

"What?"

"Chefs make things that go well with rice, right? So rice is something a chef could never do without," I explained.

"Oh—"

"Rice is amazing, you know. It can turn into so many kinds of dishes. Japanese, Chinese, European—it goes with anything, and you could eat it every day without getting tired of it. When you're sick, you make rice porridge. Then there's sushi, omrice, beef bowls, fried rice. There's not a single Japanese person who hates rice, is there?"

Mai-chan remained quiet.

"Maybe your parents named you that because they wanted you to become someone who was just like that. They put a lot of thought into your name, so you should feel proud of it." I said.

Mai protested, "But I've been teased about it ever since I was little! At preschool and at elementary school. And when I came here, Futa-kun . . ."

"But you know, it's a name no one will ever forget once they see it and hear it."

"But . . ."

"They'll remember it right away. It's a special name."

"Maybe . . ."

"Don't you think it's better than having people ask what your name is over and over?" I asked.

She didn't answer.

"I'm positive it is. You know, Mai-chan, my mom and dad are gone, too. They both died in an accident."

"Huh? Yours too?"

"That's right. But see, whenever something terrible

happens to me, there's something I always tell myself. 'I can't let this experience go to waste. I *have* to learn something from it and spring back from it so I can grow as a person.'"

Drip, drip.

And just like that, tears began pouring from Mai-chan's eyes. She must have been holding back her tears all this time.

"I-I . . ." she sobbed.

"You can cry as much as you want. You're cutting onions right now, after all."

At that, the tears welled up in Mai-chan's eyes and became unstoppable.

"Here." I handed her a towel.

"I-I'm sorry."

Mai-chan bowed her head to me as she cried.

"You don't need to apologize."

"No, I do. I acted so bad," she wailed.

"Don't worry about it."

"But Futa-kun is always talking about you,

Najika-san. He seemed so happy that you were coming. Even when everyone was shouting about getting to meet Akane Kishida-san, he was the only one who didn't care."

"Huh?"

"He said you were really good at cooking and the cream puffs you make are delicious. He talked about it all the time. But I—I'm good at cooking, too! And it hurt my feelings so much," she said.

"Oh, so that's what's going on!"

"Huh?"

"So you like Futa?"

Mai-chan turned bright red. "N-no I don't! That's not what I . . ."

"I understand. In that case, just leave it to me," I assured her.

"Huh?"

4

"Did everyone do their homework this morning like you were supposed to?" I asked the kids in the kitchen, after we'd eaten an amazingly good curry.

"Yeah!"

"Like we were supposed to!"

"Then you can go play until your afternoon snack."

"Yay!"

A cheer went up from the children.

"Who wants to find cicada shells? Daichi Kitazawa-sensei will be your guide!"

"Hiya!" Daichi stood up and they applauded.

"Who wants to press flowers and decorate their hair with wildflowers? Anju Takanashi-sensei will be your guide!"

"Hello, everyone." This time Anju stood up. Again, there was loud applause.

"Okay, Daichi, Anju, Akane—can you take care of the kids? I'm going to stay here."

"What? I'm not going! Sunburns are strictly forbidden!" Akane yelled.

"Aww, Akane-chan! Please!"

The girls surrounded her.

"They're right. Why did you even come to Hokkaido, Akane? Go enjoy the great outdoors!"

"But—"

"Everybody! It's hot outside today, so I made some homemade sherbet for your snack! Come back at three o'clock!" I said.

"Okay! We'll be back."

"Oh, Futa, Mai-chan? Just a second." I called the two of them back as they were about to leave.

"What is it?"

"See, the yummy sherbet I made is in the freezer."

"Uh-huh?"

"But in order to make smooth, delicious sherbet, you have to stir it up every thirty minutes to fill it with air," I explained.

"Why?"

"If you don't stir it up real good, it makes little lumps of ice and gets all gritty."

"Oh-h-h."

"But I have to go help Hagio-sensei with some work. So I'm putting *you two* in charge of stirring it."

"What? Not again!"

"Thanks! It's a big help!" I smiled.

"H-hey, Najika!"

■ ■ ■

It was a hot, summer afternoon.

I peeked into the kitchen and saw Futa and Mai-chan, still utterly silent.

"Najika," Hagio-sensei whispered in a low voice. "I'm sure those two would like to go play, too."

"I know."

"Then why did you give them something so time-consuming to do?" she asked.

"Because they need time to get to know each other."

"I see."

"Besides, no matter how delicious the treat I offer them, they won't enjoy it if they're fighting, will they?"

"That's so like you, Najika." Hagio-sensei smiled at me.

■ ■ ■

In the meantime, the two had begun a halting conversation, as if they could no longer stand the silence.

"Sherbet takes a lot of work, huh?" Futa said.

"Yeah."

"But you're done eating it so fast."

"That's true," she answered.

"Uh, hey Mai."

"What?"

"I-I'm sorry I teased you . . . about your name."

"Huh?"

"I think Mai is a great name. Really."

"Really?"

"Man, it's so hot today," Futa said, turning his back on Mai-chan.

He flapped the collar of his shirt.

Heehee. How funny. Futa's trying to look cool.

But his cheeks turned red as he looked away.

Oh, so that's what it is! Futa has a crush on Mai-chan, too. That's why he was always teasing her!

I'm glad they patched things up. That is one relief.

Hagio-sensei nodded with a smile, too.

Outside the window, sunflowers were blooming. Thunderclouds floated in the blue sky like whipped cream. The song of cicadas. The brilliant sunlight.

Very soon a cool, sweet, incredibly delicious treat would be ready. I really was impatient for snack-time. I wanted to taste the sharp coolness of the sherbet right now. I wanted to eat with them—with the people I love most, whenever possible.

■ ■ ■

"See ya!"

As soon as snack-time was over, Futa and Mai-chan ran out into the brilliant summer sun.

If they could be just a little nicer to each other, I was sure they had a happy future ahead of them.

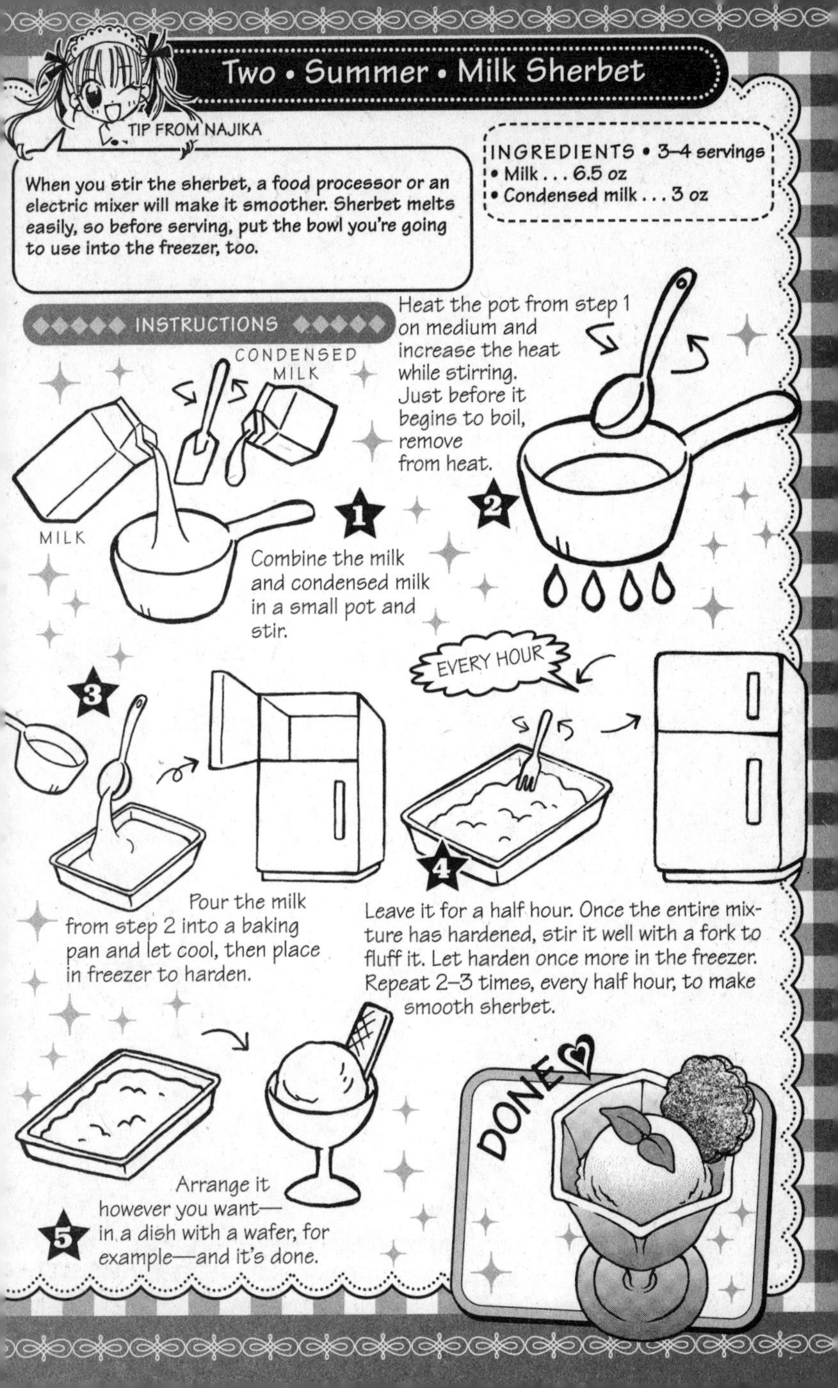
Two • Summer • Milk Sherbet
TIP FROM NAJIKA
When you stir the sherbet, a food processor or an electric mixer will make it smoother. Sherbet melts easily, so before serving, put the bowl you're going to use into the freezer, too.
INGREDIENTS • 3–4 servings
• Milk . . . 6.5 oz
• Condensed milk . . . 3 oz
INSTRUCTIONS
CONDENSED MILK
MILK
1
Combine the milk and condensed milk in a small pot and stir.
2
Heat the pot from step 1 on medium and increase the heat while stirring. Just before it begins to boil, remove from heat.
3
Pour the milk from step 2 into a baking pan and let cool, then place in freezer to harden.
EVERY HOUR
4
Leave it for a half hour. Once the entire mixture has hardened, stir it well with a fork to fluff it. Let harden once more in the freezer. Repeat 2–3 times, every half hour, to make smooth sherbet.
5
Arrange it however you want—in a dish with a wafer, for example—and it's done.
DONE

Fall / automne

Recipe Three • Najika and Icebox Cookies

■

1

■

"I think Kazami would be great as our president for the school festival!"

"Second!"

"I agree, too!"

"What? Me?"

Clap-clap-clap. There was unanimous applause in homeroom.

Really? Can someone like me handle it?

"So will you do it, Kazami-san?" Nagano-kun, the class representative, asked me.

"Sure! I, Najika Kazami, will do my best!"

■ ■ ■

It was early in the afternoon of a bright autumn day. The sky was broad and sharply blue.

I stretched my arms high over my head in the clear

sunlight and took in a deep breath. It felt like good things were going to happen this semester!

"They picked me to be president of the school festival!"

Daichi and Akane looked dubious when I told them that in the Fujita Diner.

"Why are you so happy?" Akane asked coldly.

"Because everyone picked me."

"They're just pushing off an unpleasant chore on you, you know," she said.

Daichi seemed disgruntled, too. "Everyone's looking ahead to the end of the semester and they just want to study."

"But . . . I think there are some kids who picked me because I'd be good at it. So I'm going to do my best!" I promised.

"You are so innocent!"

"Hmph. . . ."

"It doesn't bother you?"

"Well . . ."

"Why don't you say something?"

"I guess."

While I was thinking . . .

"Najika!"

Anju came into the Fujita Diner. "My parents brought you this from Paris."

"Oh wow, *chocolat*! It looks so expensive. It's really for me? I love it!"

"They said you've been a big help with my grandmother. Daichi-kun, Akane, you have some, too," Anju offered.

"But the cheesecake wasn't right, either. I'm sorry I haven't gotten close to finding it yet. . . . Does she have any other hints?"

"I came to report on that! My grandmother told me a little while ago that it was a baked dessert," Anju said.

"A baked dessert? Hmm. Maybe I've been too focused on cakes."

"Huh?"

"There are still lots of other baked desserts, like crumbly white cookies or macaroons," I explained.

"Ooh, I see."

"Okay, I'll research a little bit more. Oh!"

"What is it?"

"I just had a great idea! What if I turned my class into a cookie bakery? That could be our theme for the school festival. That way, I could hit two birds with one stone and do the class's work at the same time as my experiments for your grandma's dessert."

"Ooh! Najika's cookie bakery, huh? That sounds fun! Everybody loved those Christmas cookies you made in sixth grade."

Yes—the first Christmas after I'd come to this school. I dressed up like Santa Claus and handed out star-shaped cookies to everyone.

Cookies were connected with happy childhood memories for me. The cookies that Mom would bake for me. The aroma of butter spreading through the room, and everyone in my family smiling.

I wonder why homemade sweets bring me such joy, joy like the sun is shining into my heart?

And cookies aren't hard to make, even for total beginners. If everyone in class baked cookies together, I was sure they would all grow closer.

I was getting excited when Akane said,

"It looks like Najika really doesn't have any complaints, Daichi."

Oh. We'd been in the middle of a conversation. As soon as the subject of sweets comes up, I tend to get lost in daydreams.

"That's 'cause as long as Najika has sweets, all her problems get better." Daichi laughed with a hint of resignation.

"Nah, it's more like, as long as she has food!" Fujita-san suddenly sprang up from the sofa. "You don't know about that, do you, Anju? The legend of Najika's appetite."

"The legend of her appetite?" Anju's face held a blank look.

"Hey, don't tell her about that!"

"She can polish off an entire box of tangerines," Fujita-san went on. "She can manage fifty meat dumplings in thirty minutes!"

"That's not that much, you guys!" I protested.

"A hundred pieces of sushi is nothing to her." This time it was Daichi.

"What! Th-that many?" Anju was shocked.

"Hey! Of course not! They're exaggerating!" I argued.

"No, I was with you at the all-you-can-eat sushi bar, so I know. Najika polished off all the rice in the restaurant and made the old guy in charge cry." Daichi laughed.

"Hmph."

It's true that I do eat a lot, but . . . they didn't need to tell an idealistic young girl like Anju about that. Hmmmph. They made me sound like a monster!

"Don't be shocked, Anju."

"I'm not. You're really amazing, Najika."

And then Anju clasped her hands tightly in front of her.

"It makes me respect you *even more.*"

"Uh-oh. There's another crazy one now." Fujita-san fell back down onto the sofa.

"A follower of the Church of Najika."

Akane was amazed, too.

But Anju smiled at me with her cream-puff smile.

"Nuh-uh. I think Anju might be the strongest one of all. . . ."

2

"Wow! Even I made one!"

It was a week later, after school. And Najika's cookie class was in session in the Fujita Diner!

My class had decided to do a cookie bakery for the festival just like I'd suggested. And today five girls from the class who'd been interested in making cookies were participating.

The other kids had all hurried off to their clubs or cram schools, as if they were leaving it all to me . . . but still!

Today I was teaching them how to make icebox cookies. These don't need a cookie cutter, so you can use all the dough without wasting any.

You mix butter, sugar, flour, and egg yolks together, then shape it into a circular or rectangular log.

Once it hardens in the freezer, you cut it with a kitchen knife and then bake.

"Cookies are so simple, Kazami-san."

"I know! If you add cocoa, they have a chocolate flavor, or you can add nuts or seeds, and make all sorts of designs of your own," I said.

"I want to add green tea to mine!"

"Maybe coconut would be good, too."

"Can I use two to make a jam sandwich cookie?"

Wow, what a great atmosphere. Everyone was getting into it!

"What kind of cookie are you going to make, Kazami-san?"

"I'm thinking of making custom cookies."

"What do you mean?"

"Well, everyone's tastes are different, right? The size, the shape, the flavor, the decoration—I'll make every single one of them different. Original, one-of-a-kind cookies."

"That's great!"

"Can I order one now, then?"

"Seriously?"

"I want it to be cinnamon-flavored and shaped like a dog, because Nagano-kun's family has a miniature dachshund." The girl's face turned red.

"Huh? Nagano-kun from our class?"

"Yeah. I want to ask him to dance with me at the final night ball. But it's still a secret."

"The ball . . ."

"Good idea! Make one for me, too, Kazami-san!"

"Me, too!"

All of a sudden, everyone's eyes were glistening.

Dance with me, huh?

The last day of the school festival, there's a dance in the assembly hall. It had become a tradition for couples to dance the very last song together. That's why everyone was in a flutter now.

The rumors about who was dancing with whom would spread through the school.

And for people who had a crush, this was their big opportunity to confess their feelings, and for everyone to be confessed to.

"That's a great idea, Kazami-san! Crush cookies. Those'll sell really well!"

"Yeah, it could be good."

"So who are you going to dance with, Kazami-san?"

"Huh?"

"Daichi-kun? Or maybe Seiya-kun?"

"What?!" I cried.

Everyone looked at me at once.

"That must be so nice. You're friends with two of the coolest guys in school."

"I-it's not like that!" I demurred.

"Oh, then can I invite Daichi-kun?"

"Me too! I want to dance with Daichi-kun!"

"I prefer Seiya-kun."

"What!"

I was speechless. I had no idea Daichi and Seiya were so popular. . . .

■ ■ ■

The time melted away. Soon we were throwing ourselves into last-minute preparations for the school festival.

Classes, of course, were canceled. At Seika Academy, the middle school and high school put on a joint festival, so it was a pretty big deal.

Everyone was scurrying around making preparations. The *bang-bang-bang* of hammering nails came from every direction. The sound of the brass band rehearsing. The drama club doing voice exercises. Paint, tape, and poster paints were scattered throughout the school, filling it with color.

The bustle of preparations for the festival filled me with excitement. I loved it, for some reason.

The classroom next door had been converted into a planetarium. In the classroom next to that, I heard the students were doing a play in Korean.

It all seemed so interesting. Our class had to do its best, too!

I was busily baking cookies in the Fujita Diner when a girl I didn't recognize stuck her head in.

"Excuse me, Kazami-san? Is this where we order the crush cookies?" the girl asked.

"How did you know?"

"Everyone's talking about it. Do you think you can make a cookie that looks like the face in this photo? I want his name on it, too, please." The girl took a picture of a boy out of her bag, looking embarrassed.

"Are you going to tell him how you feel?"

"Yeah. Can you make it by tomorrow?"

"Leave it to me!" I promised.

It felt like I'd become Cupid. I hoped everyone's relationships went well!

As soon as the girl left, the music teacher came in.

"Oh, sensei—" I said.

"May I place an order, too? For a crush cookie?" she asked.

"What? You want one, too?"

"Could you hold back on the sugar and make it a bitter-chocolate flavor? Apparently he doesn't like sweets."

This was crazy.

How was it gonna turn out?

And after that . . .

"Can you do it, Kazami-san?"

"Lemme order from you, too!"

There was a rush of orders at the cookie bakery before the festival. Girls and boys alike came running. I wanted to cheer, I was so happy. But this was out of control!

"Hey, Najika."

"Oh, Daichi."

"I heard the weirdest rumor. They're saying that if you invite someone to the ball on the last night with one of your cookies, it'll go perfectly," he said.

"How is that getting around?"

"It's word of mouth. This is how urban legends get started, you know."

"Urban legends? Don't blow it out of proportion."

"The number of orders is incredible, though," Daichi said, looking at my notes.

"What am I going to do? I don't know if I can I actually make them all."

"Do you have enough ingredients?"

"I'm running out of flour! And butter. And sugar, and eggs!"

Daichi laughed. "Okay. I'll help you go shopping."

We both got onto Daichi's bicycle and set out. We bought a big bag of flour, and some butter, sugar, and eggs.

On the way back, we tied the bags to the bike's seat and Daichi pushed the bike.

"You wanna take a break?"

"Okay," I agreed.

We stopped in a park and sat beside each other on a bench. Daichi went to buy some lattes, and we drank them together.

The autumn air was as sharp as glass. We heard the rustling noise of footsteps through fallen leaves.

Daichi and I had met in the autumn of sixth grade. Right after I'd transferred into this school. A lot had happened since then. But whenever I was in trouble, Daichi had always helped me.

The city was humid and had a pensive air. I took in a deep breath and felt as if the colors of autumn were seeping through my entire body.

Daichi had been with me through it all. His round eyes. His willful lips. He was pretty cute, when I looked at him like this.

I wondered if Daichi would confess his feelings to me or ask me to dance with him? The thought made my heart swell suddenly.

"Najika? Is something wrong?"

"Nothing. Thank you for your help today, Daichi. You really saved me," I said.

"What's up? You're so serious all of a sudden." Daichi laughed, peering into my eyes.

His face was right in front of me and my heart pounded loudly. Oh, no—my cheeks turned red.

I turned my face away quickly.

"W-what are you doing for the ball, Daichi?"

"What do you mean?"

"You're not going to dance?"

"Are you kidding? Of course not! I would never do something that embarrassing!" Daichi rejected the idea immediately.

Oh. So he's not going to dance? It was kind of a relief. But it was also kind of a letdown. . . .

I glanced up and, past the grove of trees in the park, I saw the early evening moon shining.

3

■

"Wow! This cookie is *so* cute!"

"Good luck with your confession of love!"

"Thanks!"

Everyone was smiling as I handed out the cookies people had ordered. Each bundle was tied up with ribbons.

A lot of people had requested heart-shaped cookies. They were decorated adorably with red or pink or white frosting.

It was a perfect autumn Saturday. The sky was clear and blue. It was the day of Seika Academy's school festival.

There were tons of people crowding inside the school. My own classroom had been completely transformed into an adorable cookie bakery.

The boys had worked hard on the interior and the decorations were done in a homey country style. There were rows of baskets, and inside were cookies, wrapped up and tied with a ribbon. We had even set up a café nook in one corner.

A crowd of customers had come and it was a big success. Everyone was busy.

"Oh, Anju! Over here!"

"Najika!" Anju had come to see me.

"Here's a snowball cookie. It's dusted with powdered sugar, and it's crunchy and fluffy. Give this to your grandmother," I offered.

"It looks delicious! Thank you so much!"

"I made one for you, too. Try it."

"Oh—"

"What is it?" I asked.

"Um, I'll pass for today."

"Why?"

"I've been eating cake with my grandmother constantly, and the skirt of my school uniform feels tighter. I'm on a diet until tomorrow," she explained.

"What's tomorrow?"

"The ball. . . . There's someone I want to invite, so . . ." Anju said in a whisper.

"Really?!"

"Can I order a cookie from you, too, Najika?"

"Of course. But just a second! You have a crush on someone?"

Anju's cheeks flushed and she nodded. "Well, it's not a crush exactly. I just like him because I think he's cool."

"I had no idea! I suppose anyone would say okay if a cute girl like you confessed to them. But how long have you liked him?"

"Since spring, maybe? But I don't want to go out with him or anything. There's no way we could. I just daydream about it. It'll be enough to dance with him at the ball."

"So who is it?"

Anju didn't answer.

"Is it a boy from the Special Class?"

"No," she demurred.

"In the high school?"

"It's not like that . . ."

"Really? Who is it?"

"He's . . . not a student," she admitted.

"A teacher?!"

"No."

"Huh?"

"It's someone you know really well. . . . Um, please make it like this." Anju turned bright red and handed me a white paper.

The design of her custom-made cookie was drawn on it.

What was this? A chef's hat?

"Wha-a-a-at?! No way!"

I was taken aback.

"Oh God! I'm so embarrassed!" Anju turned even redder and ran out of the room.

No way. No way.

F-Fujita-san?!

How could something so outrageous happen in the real world? A lovely young girl like Anju? And an old guy like him?! How can she like *him*?

"No way!" My cry echoed through the classroom.

■ ■ ■

"Me? Dance at the ball on closin' night? With Anju? A-are you kiddin'?" Fujita-san wailed in the Fujita Diner. "A chill goes down my spine just thinkin' about it. I don't wanna do it!"

"No one's saying you have to go out with her. Just dance one song with her," I chided.

"Of course they're not sayin' that! If I was datin' a middle schooler, that would be a crime! They're gonna arrest me!" Fujita-san shouted.

"I don't want to ask you to do this, either. I just want to make Anju's wish come true!"

"Anju has some pretty eccentric interests."

Akane made a face of open disgust. "What's so great about this old guy?"

When I'd learned the astonishing truth, I'd hurried to consult with Akane. And the two of us had come to ask this favor of Fujita-san.

"I suppose she saw him cooking at the flower-viewing party and somehow got the idea that he was amazing."

Akane let out a sigh at my answer. "Anju has always had a father complex, you know. She doesn't have the slightest interest in the boys in her class."

"I just won't come to school tomorrow!" he cried.

"Don't be so mean, Fujita-san! You can do that much for her at least!" I said.

"I refuse. Not even if my life depended on it!"

Then Akane asked in a low, menacing voice, "Does

that mean you won't care if I expose your embarrassing past, Fujita-san?"

"Huh?"

Akane showed the screen of her cellphone to me and Fujita-san.

"H-hey! That's . . . Y-you wouldn't."

Is that a band photo? I thought, then realized that Fujita-san was the lead singer! His hair was long, and he even had makeup on! And he was dressed up like a frilly prince!

"Bwahahaha!" I burst out laughing.

"I-I was the lead singer of a glam rock band in high school!" Fujita-san's eyes boggled. "Akane! How did you get that?"

"Your dad took a picture of the album, and he sent the picture to my phone. We explained the situation to him and he was happy to cooperate," she said.

"Th-that rotten old man!"

"If you don't dance with Anju, I'll put this up all over school!" Akane threatened.

"Wow, Akane! You're awesome!"

I gave her a round of heartfelt applause.

"That's the one part of my past that I never wanted anyone to find out about, and my old man exposed it!" he cried.

"Come on, Fujita-san. Anju has been through a lot, having to help her grandmother, and with her parents talking about divorce. Don't you want to help her have fun for a change?" Akane asked in an unusually earnest tone of voice. I was touched.

She had some good qualities after all.

"What about you, Akane? Who are you going to dance with? Seiya?" I asked her teasingly.

"No way! In my case, the boys who want to dance with me get in line. But shouldn't you be more worried about yourself, Najika?"

"What?"

"Are you all alone? Aren't you going to come? Everyone else is desperately looking for someone to go with. But you're taking your sweet time."

It was true. . . . I did want to go to a dance at least once to see what it was like. . . .

But there was no one to invite me.

Hmph. I am so unpopular!

4

■

"I'm exhausted," I sighed.

The orders had come one after another and there'd been no time to rest. The second day of the festival was over. Now all that was left was the ball.

"Thank you, Kazami-san."

"You did a great job!"

Everyone in the class came to congratulate me all at once.

Some kids were even honest enough to admit: "We pushed you into it, but you did a great job. I'm impressed."

I'm glad . . . I'm so glad I took on the job after all! There'd been a distance between us, and I felt like I'd grown closer to everyone in the class.

But since I'd spent two whole days on my feet baking cookies nonstop, my back ached. My tension dissolved and all the strength rushed out of my body. I was wiped out, and I slumped down to sit on the floor.

Everyone else had gone to the dance, and no one was left in the classroom. The trees outside the window had started to turn red. Some leaves danced in the wind.

Grrgle.

My stomach grumbled, which reminded me that I'd hardly eaten anything since that morning.

Why did I feel so sad when I was hungry?

I hugged my knees to my chest, and just then . . .

. . . someone held a heart-shaped cookie out in front of me.

Huh?

A crush cookie?

When I looked up in surprise, I saw Daichi standing there.

What? I was so shocked I couldn't think of anything to say.

Thump, thump.

There was only the sound of my heart pounding.

"What's this?"

"I asked someone in your class for it and they made it for me on the sly," he said.

"When did you—"

The sound of my pounding heart flowed out into the dusky classroom. My heart squeezed painfully tight.

Daichi crouched down and his face was right in front of me . . .

"I-is this an invitation to the dance . . . or something?"

"Of course not."

"B-but . . ."

"You worked really hard, right? And everyone in your class supported you. It's an apology for saying such mean things before," he said.

"Oh. You didn't have to worry about that."

"Well, I figured as long as you have food, you're happy."

"Then this is from me," I said, taking a cookie out of a pocket in my uniform. "I wanted to give this to you, too."

I'd added cocoa to make a brown, circular cookie, and used icing to make it look like a basketball. It was in a clear plastic bag and tied with a leaf-brown ribbon.

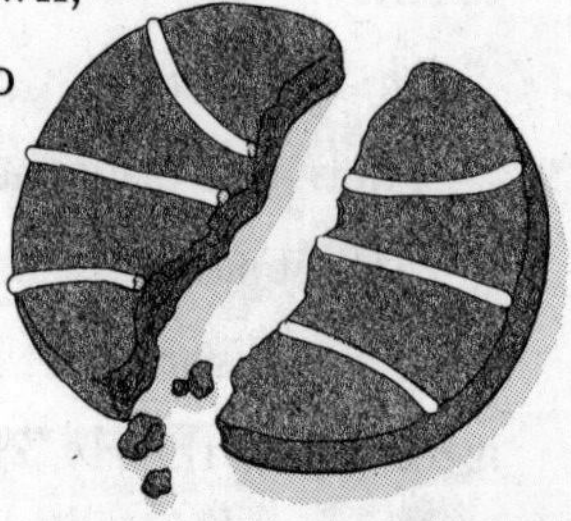

"A basketball, huh?"

"I like you best when you're playing basketball," I said.

"Thanks."

As I spoke, Daichi slowly untied the ribbon. Then he took the cookie out and broke it in two. He pressed half of it into my mouth.

"I'm going to get serious about basketball again."

"Really?"

"Yeah. Hey, this is really good. It tastes like chocolate."

"You're right! This is great!"

"You're not supposed to say that about yourself." Daichi smirked.

Outside the window it was already twilight. The setting sun painted the school yard red. A sweet melody came from the hall. Daichi offered me his hand.

"Let's go," he said.

"Huh? Where?"

"I'm a really bad dancer, though."

My heart leapt into my throat. *Seriously?* Daichi was going to the dance with *me*?

"A-are you sure?"

I couldn't believe it.

"Akane got mad at me. She told me I should at least invite you."

I hadn't expected to hear that and my eyes teared up.

"Hey, silly, don't cry about that."

"But . . . but . . ."

A tear rolled down my cheek. Daichi's outstretched hand covered my own. These feelings were invisible, but important.

Our joined hands communicated them perfectly. We only ever said mean things to each other.

But my eyes couldn't lie. I don't know when, but at some point my eyes had started seeking Daichi out. I wanted to see him a lot more.

He was awkward and stubborn and wasn't always nice. But really, his heart was purer than anyone else's.

I knew that for sure. I felt like Cinderella heading to the ball just then.

I was dressed in the same school uniform as always, but hey—could Daichi see the gown of excitement that I wore now?

■ ■ ■

Everyone was already gathered at the hall.

Anju seemed happy. Fujita-san seemed sulky and embarrassed.

Akane and Seiya were teasing them.

"Oh! Najika's here!"

"And hey, Daichi's with her."

We ran up to our circle of friends.

The familiar hall seemed to be sparkling, like I was seeing it through a special filter. I was sure that was because Daichi was beside me.

"The urban legend was true after all," Daichi whispered.

"What?"

"My invitation was a huge success," Daichi said, and I burst into laughter.

Three • Autumn • Icebox Cookies

TIP FROM NAJIKA

This is a convenient recipe because if you just make the cookie dough and put it in the freezer, you can have freshly baked cookies whenever you want. You should use it up within one month.

INGREDIENTS • 16–18 cookies

- **Unsalted butter . . . 1/3 cup**
- **Granulated sugar . . . 3 tbsp**
- **Egg yolk . . . 1**
- **Cake flour . . . 1 1/4 cup**

INSTRUCTIONS

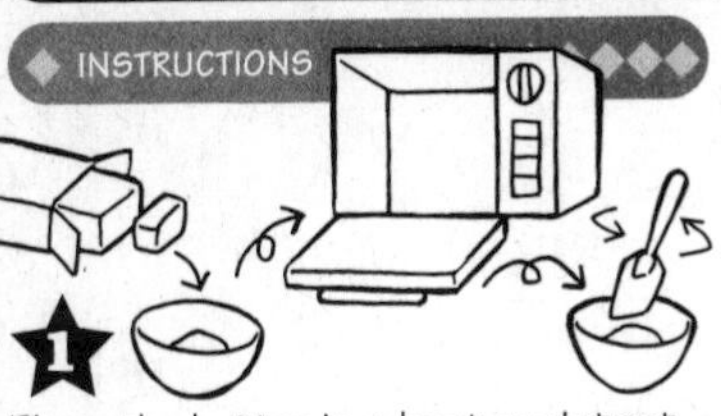

1. Place the butter in a heat-resistant dish and heat in the microwave for 20 to 30 seconds until it becomes semi-liquid. If you watch it and heat for 10 seconds at a time, that works better. Pour into a bowl and stir well with a rubber spatula.

2. Add the granulated sugar and mix well, then add the egg yolk and mix well.

3. Add sifted flour and stir using a cutting motion, folding it into the dough.

4. When the dough becomes yellow and holds its shape, put it on a cutting board and roll it into a log about 2 inches in diameter. Wrap this in wax paper and chill in the freezer for 30 minutes.

5. Remove the wax paper and cut the dough into circles about half an inch thick. Arrange these on a cookie sheet greased or lined with parchment paper, with about one inch between them.

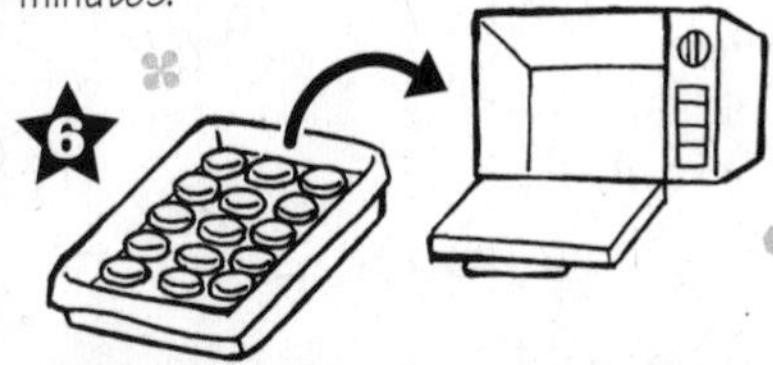

6. Bake for 20 to 25 minutes in an oven preheated to 325°F. Adjust the time to match your particular oven! Cool completely on a wire rack, and they're done.

Winter / hiver

Recipe Four • Najika and Angel Food Cake

■

1

■

"Sorry to keep you waiting! The vanilla soufflé is done!"

The weak, pure sunlight of winter shone in through the window to the sunroom of Anju's house, full of greenery.

Today I had borrowed the kitchen at Anju's house and made a soufflé.

"How is it?" I prompted the old lady, who wore a shawl on her shoulders.

"Very good, thank you." Her eyes were shining.

"Then that's—!"

"But this isn't right, either," she said.

". . . It isn't?" I sighed.

My hopes were dashed. Back in the kitchen, my shoulders slumped.

"I'm sorry, Anju."

"Oh, don't apologize, Najika."

"But your grandmother asked me to do this in spring, and we've been through the summer and autumn and now somehow it's winter. The year is almost over. It's going to be Christmas soon!"

Anju said nothing.

"I really wonder what I should do. I'm almost out of ideas. Or maybe I'm just not good enough."

"It's not your fault, Najika," Anju said. "You know, Najika, lately I've been thinking . . ."

"Hm?"

"Maybe there really is no such cake," she said.

"What?"

"My grandmother isn't herself. Maybe it doesn't actually exist."

"Maybe you're right. . . ." I admitted.

"The year is almost over, so I think this month should be the last."

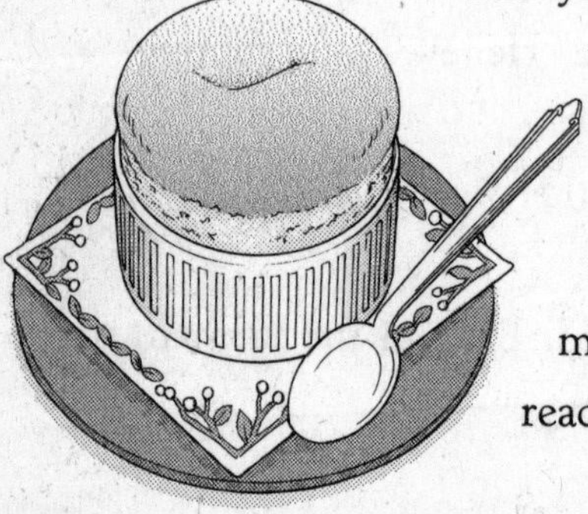

"Huh?"

"We can't put you to any more trouble than we already have, Najika."

"But Anju—"

I didn't want to give up. But to be honest, I didn't know what to do or what I could make for her anymore.

"I'll tell my grandmother. Don't worry about it, Najika."

"But . . ."

I returned to the sunroom with Anju, feeling conflicted, when . . .

"Thank you for always making such delicious cakes."

. . . the old lady offered me a small white box.

"Huh?"

"It's a bit early, but it's a Christmas present for you." It was tied up with a silver ribbon. "Go on, open it."

I untied the ribbon and peeled back the wrapping paper, then opened the box.

"Oh, how adorable! It's an angel necklace!"

The silver angel gleamed.

"It's from Paris."

"Angel . . . angel . . . oh, it's cake for an angel!" I guessed suddenly.

"Cake for an angel?" Anju asked me.

"Yes! It's a cake for Anju!"

"What?"

■ ■ ■

The next week, there was a Christmas party at Anju's house.

The attendees were all people I recognized as guests from the flower-viewing party. The dessert was again being prepared by the four of us: Fujita-san, Daichi, Akane, and me.

A bright fire burned in the hearth of the spacious living room. The Christmas tree reached the ceiling and was covered with blinking lights. With laughter and light chitchat filling the entire house, a more pleasant atmosphere could not be imagined.

It was almost impossible to believe it was the same house as the one I'd first visited.

A home reflects the feelings of the people living there, I guess. I was glad for Anju.

Today even her wheelchair-bound grandmother was radiant in an evening gown, and Anju's mother and father stood close beside her.

Since it was winter and cold outside, we had filled the menu with warm baked apples and pudding, freshly baked biscuits, chestnut tarts, and many other kinds of desserts. We also prepared hot tea and coffee, and warm wine for the adults.

The tablecloths and napkins were coordinated in Christmas colors of red and green.

Then Anju started playing "Silent Night" on the piano.

At that signal, Fujita-san appeared, dressed up as Santa Claus in a red robe and white beard.

"Merry Christmas!"

A cheer of excitement went up as Santa Claus appeared.

Fujita-san headed toward Anju's grandmother, who sat in the very center of the room.

"I've brought you a cake for an angel."

It was a chiffon cake decorated with white frosting: an angel food cake.

The old lady's eyes sparkled.

"That *is* an angel's cake, isn't it?"

Anju's mother had taken over playing the piano, and Anju came over to me to listen.

"What makes that an angel's cake?" Daichi asked, beside me.

"It's called that because it only uses egg whites. It's a light, fluffy cake decorated pure white."

"It's like snow—how perfect for Christmas."

Akane smiled, too.

"It's a traditional cake that's been made in America since the nineteenth century."

"Wow."

"Plus, in French, 'angel food cake' is called *gâteau d'ange blanc.*"

"Ange?"

"That's right. *Gâteau* is 'cake.' *Blanc* is 'white.' And *ange* means 'angel.'"

"That's my name. My grandmother gave it to me. . . ." Anju whispered.

"Is this the cake you were looking for, ma'am?" I asked, approaching the old lady.

"Yes, this is it! I wanted to taste this again!"

The old lady smiled.

"You did it!"

Anju clutched my hands.

"I'm glad I didn't give up."

"Definitely!"

"Now let's eat!"

I cut into the cake with a knife.

"I love cutting up an entire cake for everyone to eat."

Anju beamed.

"I know! I love it, too."

"Don't you feel like you're serving everyone a piece of happiness?"

Let's cut a cake into many portions and eat together. Let's all share in the happiness on Christmas day.

"Here you go."

I held out a white plate with cake on it. Anju's grandmother picked up a piece of the cake with a fork and brought it to her lips.

"How is it?"

"Yes, this is the taste. It's fluffy and sweet and melts away on the tongue. But . . ."

My heart skipped.

"Something is wrong . . ."

"It is?!"

2

"What the heck? It's wrong again?" Fujita-san let out a sigh and yanked his white beard off.

Just then . . .

"Oh my!" The old lady's eyes widened. "So it was you!"

"Huh?"

"I didn't know you were here. I've been looking for you for so long. So long—" The old lady looked as if she were about to cry. "Where have you been all this time?"

"Huh? Me? Are you talkin' to me?" Fujita-san was rattled. "W-why are you actin' like that?"

"Because I love you, of course!"

Wha-a-a-a-at?

Anju, Daichi, Akane, and I all looked from the old lady to Fujita-san and back again.

Wha-a-at? W-what was happening?

"What did she just say?" I asked Akane just to be sure.

"She definitely said she loves him," Akane said with a nod.

"A-are you serious?" Daichi was shocked.

"Anju?"

I looked at Anju, but she was the only one who still had a straight face.

"Uh, well . . ." Fujita-san fumbled. "I . . . I'm going to get changed."

"That's all right. You look wonderful as Santa."

"Oh, but—"

"Don't go, Ghent-san!"

The old lady clung to Fujita-san. Everybody's eyes turned on her.

"Who's Ghent-san?"

"That's my grandfather's name," Anju said softly. "Fujita-san actually does resemble my grandfather when he was young. I guess that's why I liked Fujita-san, too."

"Huh. So Anju has a grandpa complex, not a father complex," Akane murmured.

"So your grandmother is mistaking Fujita-san for your grandfather?"

"It looks that way . . ."

Anju drooped. "Lately her memory loss has been terrible . . ."

Her shoulders were shaking. "You finally came to see me! I'm so happy!"

The old lady sounded thrilled, her cheeks as flushed as a schoolgirl's. Her eyes were sparkling.

"I-I'm just going to go change. I'll be back. Excuse me!" Fujita-san rushed out of the room.

As soon as he left, the sparkle in the old lady's expression faded visibly.

Anju and I rushed out of the room and caught Fujita-san in the hallway.

"Fujita-san, wait!"

"Uh, I-I'm going home. The old lady's actin' weird."

"Please, Fujita-san. Just play along with her." Anju bowed to Fujita-san.

"Wha-a-at? What's goin' on?"

"She thinks that you're my dead grandfather," she explained.

"Me?"

"My grandmother loved him. They had a passionate romance while he was alive. Ever since he passed away a year ago, my grandmother has been getting weaker and weaker, and now she's like this—"

"So that's what happened . . ."

My heart felt deathly cold.

"She's said that she wants to see my grandfather again so many times. She's missed him very much. So please grant her her wish, just for today. Please."

"Please, Fujita-san. Do it for me, too!" I also bowed to him.

My heart ached. The gentlest part of my soul felt pained, as if someone were squeezing it.

■ ■ ■

"Grandmother? Grandfather's come back from changing."

Anju and I brought Fujita-san, who had changed into a suit, back to her grandmother.

The old lady's lifeless expression brightened like flipping the switch on a neon light.

"Oh! So you really did come! I'm so glad."

"I-I changed into that suit you like, F . . . Fujiko." Fujita-san was acting his heart out.

"It suits you very well. I picked it out in Paris."

"Yes, that's right, you did."

The old lady squeezed Fujita-san's hand and he smiled tensely.

Daichi and Akane were surprised by Fujita-san's performance.

But I could understand how the old lady felt. I had lost my mother and father, and I had lost Sora-san, and I had felt despair words couldn't express.

I would want to see them if I could.

I would want to see them, too.

The old lady had lost the man she loved and was in the grips of a sadness so deep it might shatter her body and her heart. That fact overwhelmed me and my heart ached as if it were being crushed.

"That suit . . . Kazami-san . . ."

Anju's father stood beside me. "That belonged to my father."

"Yes. Anju got it out and Fujita-san agreed to wear it."

"He really does resemble my father, dressed like that. It's as if my father were here, in his youth." Tears glistened faintly in his eyes. "It's been a long time since I saw my mother look so happy."

When he said that, I suddenly felt as if I were going to cry, too.

"Do you remember this cake?" The old lady held

the cake I'd given her earlier out to Fujita-san. "We ate it together, long, long ago."

So that's what it was. It was the cake she'd eaten with Anju's grandfather . . .

"Your host mother at your homestay made it for us. There were no fluffy, chiffon cakes like this in Japan at the time."

". . . Yes, that's right."

Fujita-san's awkwardness suddenly disappeared.

"We were both so surprised that a cake this delicious existed."

Anju's father explained for me: "My mother and father met in their teens at a music school in America. My father was a violinist."

As he explained, Daichi and Akane's expressions both turned serious. Everyone there held their breath and watched the old lady and Fujita-san.

"Let's eat, shall we?" The old lady took a bite of the cake.

Then Fujita-san kindly accepted the plate and fork.

He took a bite, then said, "It really is delicious when we eat it together."

The old lady's face lit up at Fujita-san's words.

"Yes. I've been wanting to taste this cake again!" Tears started to fill her eyes. "I ate this cake on our first date."

The old lady looked at me like someone waking up from a dream.

"Kazami-san!"

"Yes?"

"Thank you. This is it. This is the cake I wanted to eat!"

"Good. I'm glad."

Yes—the words Anju's grandfather had spoken must have been a confession of love.

The words "It's delicious when we eat it together" also meant "I love you."

That was it. It wouldn't have been right with any old angel food cake. Without those words, it wouldn't have worked.

If the old lady hadn't eaten it with her beloved husband, it wouldn't have been right.

That was it.

It wasn't any ingredient or any preparation method.

What the old lady had wanted to taste was a cake flavored with that declaration of love.

"I've never seen Grandmother look so happy since

Grandfather died." Tears streamed down Anju's cheeks, too.

"This has been a wonderful Christmas for my grandmother. Thank you, Najika."

"I'm sure this will make your grandmother better," I said.

"Yeah. I know it will!"

Anju's mother was leaning on her father's shoulder, crying. Her father gently hugged her mother's shoulder. I was sure that Anju's parents would be able to work things out.

And my parents in heaven—I, their daughter, had fulfilled the promise they'd made to the old lady.

This is how cake can bring people together. It can make someone smile. It can stir up emotions.

Yes—that's the job of the pastry chef.

"I feel wonderful today," the old lady said with a smile. "Perhaps I'll play the piano for a change."

"Ohh!"

"The great pianist of the past stages her comeback!"

Everyone murmured excitedly.

With Anju's help, the old lady sat down at the piano. She closed her eyes, straightened her back, and froze, as if she were waiting for something.

She gave off an incredible aura.

Everyone watched her. There was a moment of silence.

Then, *thrum*!

A passionate chord rang out.

"It's Chopin . . ."

Her long, fair fingers moved quickly and nimbly over the keys.

"Wow . . ."

Everyone held their breath.

Fujiko Takanashi, the famous pianist of years gone by, was in the room.

I don't know anything about classical music, but I instinctively understood that a performance like this was rare. All at once, the room had become a magnificent concert hall. A spotlight shining on a stage. A grand piano. A standing ovation from the sold-out audience. Unending waves of applause.

And it would be for the last time. . . .

▪ ▪ ▪

Early the next morning, the phone rang at the Fujita Diner.

"Huh?!"

Fujita-san picked up the phone, then fell silent.

He stared into space.

"What's wrong?"

A terrible sense of foreboding flashed through my heart.

"Fujiko-san is—" Fujita-san broke off. "She's dead."

"What?!"

Crash!

The plate I'd been carrying slipped out of my hands and shattered on the floor. It was like I'd been frozen; I couldn't move. Why? She had been so vibrant just last night!

3

■

The funeral was held at a nearby church the next day. Rain had been falling in a drizzle since that morning and the whole world was gray.

The four of us—Daichi, Akane, Fujita-san, and I—attended the service.

The piano performances the old lady had given in life resounded through the church.

She looked very peaceful inside her casket. She seemed like she might open her eyes at any moment. I still couldn't believe what had happened.

"I really enjoyed our afternoon teas, ma'am. I'm glad I met you." I gently laid a white flower inside the casket. "Have you found your beloved husband yet? If you see my mom or dad or Sora-san in heaven, give them my best."

As the service ended and we left the church, the rain turned into sleet, spattering us with freezing-cold moisture.

My body felt heavy somehow. It was like there was lead stuffed into my stomach.

"I'm so shocked, I still can't believe it," I murmured. "I wonder, why does everyone have to die?"

Then the sleet turned to snow. The city was frighteningly quiet.

"And you can never see them again." A tear fell down my cheek. "Like my mom, or dad, or Sora-senpai."

The cold snow fell softly on my cheek and melted.

"Or Anju's grandmother."

Tears filled my eyes.

What is death? What is it like? The people and things that are important to you get taken away somewhere.

And the people who are taken away never come back again.

Everyone dies. And some day, when I get older, I'll die, too.

The old lady's death had opened a gigantic hole in my heart, and a fierce snowstorm was blowing through it.

"Najika."

Anju came out of the church. Her breath was white in the air.

"Najika, Daichi-kun, Akane—thank you so much for coming today."

Anju bowed her head, her eyes puffy with tears.

"Thank you, too, Fujita-san. I think you made my grandmother very happy."

"No, I'm sure she's with the real old man by now, so she's forgotten about me."

Fujita-san smirked as he let out white puffs of breath.

"I'm sure the reason this happened so suddenly was that Grandfather was jealous of you, Fujita-san. And he carried Grandmother away." Anju smiled faintly, then her face twisted and she burst into tears.

"Anju . . ."

The next instant, it was as if something deep inside my body had broken, and I was bawling, too.

"Najika—I'm so glad you managed to help her taste the cake before the end." Anju wrapped her arms around my shoulders.

"So don't cry."

"But I . . . I . . . it was like being with your grandmother the way she really was, and it made me so glad."

The days I had spent with the old lady, through spring, summer, fall, and winter, I'd become like a grandchild to her.

"You know Hans Christian Andersen, don't you Najika?" Anju asked suddenly. "The one who's famous for *The Little Mermaid* and *The Little Match Girl.*"

What was Anju trying to say?

"He wrote so many children's stories, but do you know what Andersen said was the most wonderful story of all?"

I shook my head silently.

"Life." Anju smiled. " 'Life itself is the most wonderful fairy tale.' Andersen said that."

Life is a wonderful fairy tale. Each and every one of us is living the most beautiful story of all. . . . If a story has a beginning, it must have an ending. Life is the same way. That's why it's wonderful.

"I think my grandmother lived a very beautiful story. I don't think she had a single regret."

As Anju said that, her face was poised and more mature than usual. It was beautiful. "After all, you heard her playing the piano, didn't you, Najika?"

I nodded.

"My grandmother burned up the last of her life in that performance, like how a sparkler flashes extra brightly just before it burns out. I think, as a pianist, it pleased her to be able to play like that. And after I heard that performance, I made a decision," Anju declared. "I'm going to be a pianist like my grandmother."

"Anju . . ."

The spark of the old lady's life hadn't disappeared. It was still burning inside Anju. The snow started falling even harder. It drifted quietly down on everyone.

Like powdered sugar on top of an angel food cake.

4

■

"Eat this, Najika."

When we got back to the Fujita Diner, I was in a daze. A bowl of soup appeared right in front of me.

"Huh?"

"I heard you haven't eaten anything all day."

Daichi sat down across from me.

"Fujita-san told me that, so I made this."

"You did? Hey, isn't this . . . ?"

"That's right. You made this for me before, remember?"

"Onion gratin soup . . ."

"It tasted great when you made it."

Warm, white steam enveloped me.

That had been the winter of sixth grade. I remembered making the same thing for Daichi out of leftovers. I spooned it into my mouth. The melted cheese was fragrant. The well-boiled onions were sweet. And it was hot enough to burn my tongue.

". . . This really warms you up."

"Right?"

It was as if the nutrients of the soup were spreading through each and every one of my cells. I felt as if I were being revived from zero. I was comforted by the tenderness of the soup that suffused my exhausted spirit.

Oh no. Tears were welling up in my eyes again.

"Najika?"

Daichi looked into my face worriedly.

"What's wrong?"

"It's really good," I sobbed.

"Is that all? I'm glad."

"I feel like I'm coming back to life."

"I bet."

"Thank you, Daichi."

Daichi softly laid his right hand over my own. His warmth came through it.

The cure for sadness is a piece of chocolate and a friend who'll pat you on the back. Hadn't I read that in some old manga?

The food you love and the person you love: As long as you have those two things, you can go on living. Even without anything else. No matter what other trials you face. Somehow, you can fight and live on.

Night had fallen and the snow was still coming down. The snow absorbed sounds and made things almost painfully silent. All around us was a world of white gold.

But when I listened to the silence, I felt as if I could hear the old lady playing the piano somewhere.

Even the bitterest cold of winter will end eventually. Spring will come to everyone in the end.

Yes—I felt as if the old lady's performance had invigorated me, and tears welled up in my eyes again.

But my hot tears were like water dripping off melting snow as they wet my cheeks.

"I want to make sweets that move people the way the old lady's music did. I wonder if I can?"

"You can. I mean come on, you? Absolutely," Daichi declared with a bright smile like the sunlight that melts the snow.

I couldn't stop the tears from coming again. . . .

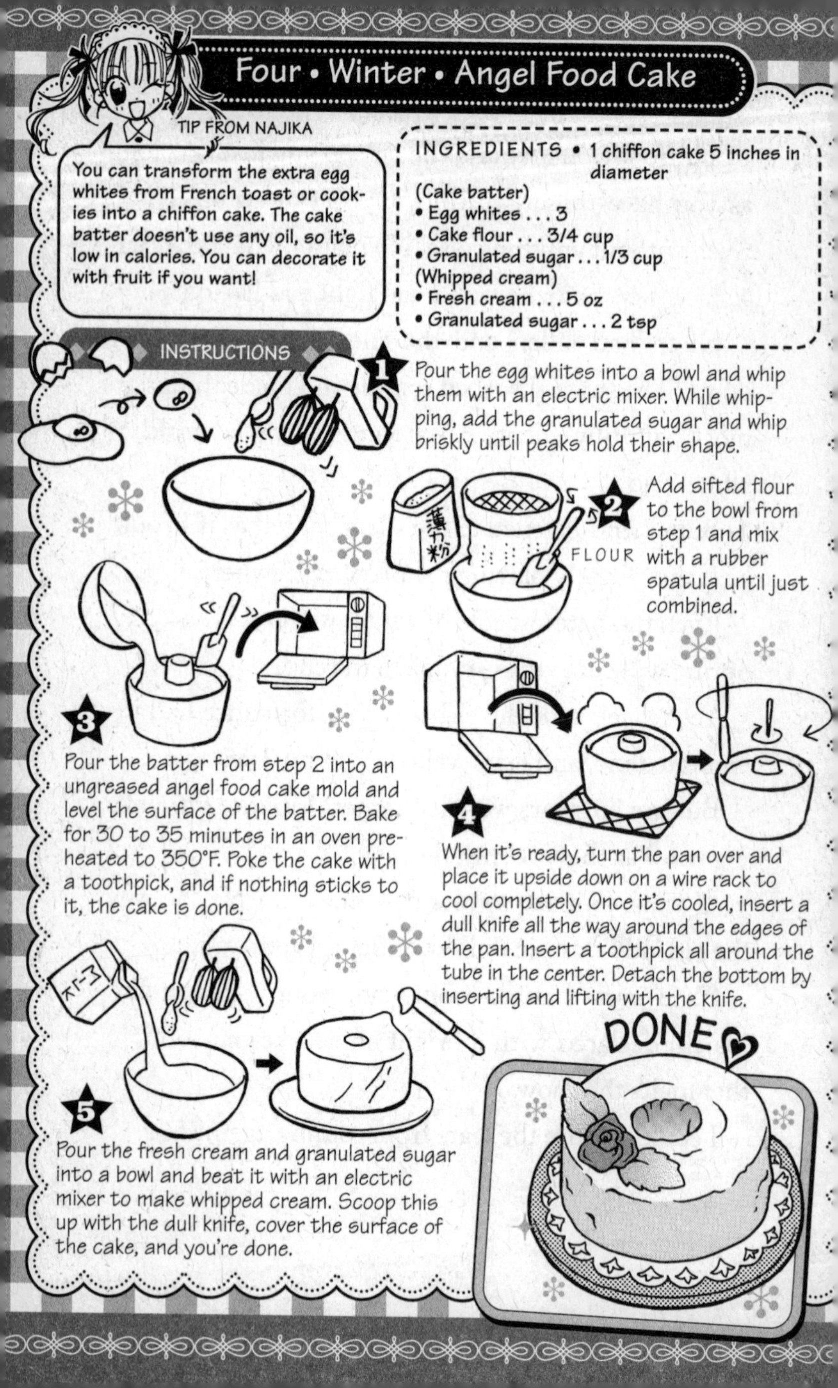
Four • Winter • Angel Food Cake
TIP FROM NAJIKA
You can transform the extra egg whites from French toast or cookies into a chiffon cake. The cake batter doesn't use any oil, so it's low in calories. You can decorate it with fruit if you want!
INGREDIENTS • 1 chiffon cake 5 inches in diameter
(Cake batter)
• Egg whites . . . 3
• Cake flour . . . 3/4 cup
• Granulated sugar . . . 1/3 cup
(Whipped cream)
• Fresh cream . . . 5 oz
• Granulated sugar . . . 2 tsp
INSTRUCTIONS
1 Pour the egg whites into a bowl and whip them with an electric mixer. While whipping, add the granulated sugar and whip briskly until peaks hold their shape.
薄力粉
FLOUR
2 Add sifted flour to the bowl from step 1 and mix with a rubber spatula until just combined.
3 Pour the batter from step 2 into an ungreased angel food cake mold and level the surface of the batter. Bake for 30 to 35 minutes in an oven preheated to 350°F. Poke the cake with a toothpick, and if nothing sticks to it, the cake is done.
4 When it's ready, turn the pan over and place it upside down on a wire rack to cool completely. Once it's cooled, insert a dull knife all the way around the edges of the pan. Insert a toothpick all around the tube in the center. Detach the bottom by inserting and lifting with the knife.
5 Pour the fresh cream and granulated sugar into a bowl and beat it with an electric mixer to make whipped cream. Scoop this up with the dull knife, cover the surface of the cake, and you're done.
DONE

About the Author

MIYUKI KOBAYASHI is the writer of the *New York Times*–bestselling manga series *Kitchen Princess,* for which she won a Kodansha Award. She lives in Japan.

About the Illustrator

NATSUMI ANDO made her debut as a manga artist in 1994 with *Headstrong Cinderella,* which won the prestigious Nakayoshi Rookie of the Year Award. Since then, she has created several popular manga series, including *Wild @ Heart, Zodiac P.I.,* and the *New York Times*–bestselling *Kitchen Princess* manga.